School Spirits

MICHAEL O. TUNNELL

BOYDS MILLS PRESS

Text copyright © 1997 by Michael O. Tunnell
Jacket illustration copyright © 1997 by Barbara J. Roman
All rights reserved

Published by Boyds Mills Press, Inc.
A Highlights Company
815 Church Street
Honesdale, Pennsylvania 18431
Printed in China

Publisher Cataloging-in-Publication Data (U.S.)

Tunnell, Michael O.
School spirits / by Michael O. Tunnell.—1st ed.
p.   cm.
Summary: When Patrick moves to a new town, he is confronted by a
ghostly boy who seeks his help.
ISBN 1-59078-376-X
Originally published: New York, Holiday House, 1997
[1. Ghosts—Fiction. 2. Schools—Fiction. 3. Horror stories.]
I. Title.
Pz7.T825Wh   1997   96–48776   CIP   AC
                              [Fic]—dc21

First Boyds Mills Press paperback edition, 2005

Visit our Web site at www.boydsmillspress.com

10 9 8 7 6 5 4 3 2

To Sydney Morganne

Chapter One

"Go on! Get out of here." Mr. Meeres pushed Patrick out the door. "You'll just be in the way until the movers finish."

Patrick glared at his father. "I wasn't in the way."

Mr. Meeres sighed. "Patrick, you were sitting in the middle of your bedroom floor reading. The house could burn down, and you wouldn't notice. The movers could smash you flat, and you'd never see them coming."

"But Dad, there's nowhere to go."

"Well, find some place. Where's your sense of adventure? New town, new neighborhood. Put the blasted book down and go find some new friends."

"Don't need any new friends," Patrick said sullenly. "I've still got Reggie."

"That makes a lot of sense, Patrick. Reggie is back in New Castle. Now get going."

The screen door slammed shut, and Mr. Meeres disappeared inside. Patrick stared after his father, then stumbled off the porch and dragged himself across the lawn. He sat down against a fence that separated his yard from the neighbors' and opened his book, barely noticing the two men wrestling a refrigerator out of the moving van.

Before Patrick could get lost in his book, a high-pitched voice from beyond the fence interrupted him. He peered through the pickets and saw a scrawny redheaded girl standing in the front yard. Her hips gyrated and her shoulders swayed as a bright green Hula-Hoop orbited her waist. "One . . . two . . . three," she droned.

The book slipped from his fingers as he watched jealously. Patrick had hurried to buy a Hula-Hoop when they'd first appeared, but had quickly discovered he couldn't keep one rotating for more than two or three turns. But this hoop flew around the girl in effortless circles. "Seventeen . . . eighteen . . . nineteen . . ."

"She can do that forever," a voice said.

Patrick peered up at a taller version of the little Hula-Hooper leaning over the fence.

"Marla's going to wear a hole right through her middle. She can do a thousand, no problem. But who'd want to, right? I'm Nairen Potter, and I guess you're Patrick Meeres."

"Yeah, how'd you know?" Patrick asked, suspiciously. He didn't bother standing up.

"Your dad's the new principal at Craven Hill. Word gets around about stuff like that. Good thing you moved here in the middle of the summer. Gives you a chance to make friends before school starts. Nothing worse than starting school without knowing any-body."

Patrick shrugged and turned back to his reading.

"What're you reading?" asked Nairen, craning to see Patrick's book. "I just love to read, especially mysteries. Nothing like a good mystery, don't you think? Or a scare-the-snot-right-out-of-you ghost story? Is that a ghost story?"

"Yeah, and I'm right at the best part," Patrick mumbled.

Nairen came around the fence and stood in front of Patrick. Refusing to look up, Patrick stared straight at two long skinny legs jutting out of pink pedal pushers. "I need to finish this," he said, waving the book slightly.

Nairen squatted to get eye level with Patrick. "Got any brothers or sisters?" she asked. "Where's your mom? Is she in the house? How about I go get my mom, and she can come over and say hi."

"No!" Patrick jumped up. Nairen tumbled backward in surprise. "No," he said more quietly. "No brothers or sisters. Just my dad."

Nairen stared silently at Patrick and then looked over at the Meeres's house.

"You won't see my mom. She's dead."

Nairen's face turned as red as her hair. She struggled to her feet and edged toward her yard. "I'm really sorry. Dad says I talk too much, and I guess he's right. I'll see you later, okay?"

"Hey, don't go," said Patrick, surprising himself. "About my mom—she died in 1953." He shrugged. "I've had five years to get used to it."

Nairen nodded. "Where'd you move from?" she asked.

"New Castle."

"Was it hard to leave?"

"Yeah." Patrick stared at the ground. "I really miss our old house. And I miss Reggie. We did everything together."

"Like my best friend, Veronica," said Nairen. "I call her Ronnie, even though her mom hates nicknames. I really miss her."

"Did she move?" Patrick closed his book.

"Ronnie's spending the summer at her grandma's. Her grandma broke her hip, so she's there to help her. She won't be home till school starts. Can I show you around? Let's go to The Corner Store first. I could really use an Eskimo Pie. My treat."

"I don't know," said Patrick, shifting uncomfortably. "My dad may need help or something. And I really should finish my book."

Nairen looked hurt. "You can't just sit around and read until September."

"I read a lot, you know."

"Well, then, you'll need to know where the library is. I'll show you . . . *after* we get ice cream."

Patrick didn't want to go, but he was down to his last unread book. "Okay," he said. "I'll ask Dad."

Mr. Meeres was holding open the screen door for the movers. Once they were inside, he noticed Patrick and Nairen standing behind him.

"Dad, this is Nairen Potter. She lives next door."

"Sure," said Mr. Meeres. "Our real estate agent told us about your family. You're Patrick's age, as I remember."

"That's right, Mr. Meeres. I'll be in your school this fall. In sixth grade. Our old principal was really sick of kids, so everyone's glad you're here. We're ready for a change, if you know what I mean. Don't you think a principal should quit if he hates kids? I sure do. Anyhow, it's nice to meet you."

Mr. Meeres blinked, an amused smile touching his lips. "Yes, I suppose a principal should like kids. It's nice to meet you, too, Nairen. I'm glad Patrick took my advice and found a friend."

Patrick scowled at his father. "Nairen wants to show me around, but I'll stay if you need me."

Mr. Meeres rolled his eyes. "Please, Nairen, get him out of my hair. Here, give me your book." Just then a sickening crash came from inside the house. "Go!" he yelled to Patrick as he dove through the doorway.

"Hey, Marla," Nairen called. "If mom asks, I went to Mr. Chin's store with Patrick. And to the library. Oh, Patrick, meet Marla. Marla, this is Patrick."

Marla stared into space and continued her relentless Hula-Hooping: ". . . three hundred fifty . . . three hundred fifty-one . . . three hundred fifty-two . . .

"Did she hear you?" asked Patrick as they walked along the sidewalk.

"Oh, she heard me, all right. Marla doesn't let anything break her concentration. Dad says that if Marla would concentrate on schoolwork like she does the Hula-Hoop, she'd be another Albert Einstein."

Turning left at the first intersection, Nairen led Patrick to a small white building huddled on one of the street corners. A tin sign on the roof announced in bold green letters: THE CORNER STORE. After the bright sunlight, it seemed dark and cool inside. Patrick breathed in the old-fashioned smell of oiled wooden floors.

Nairen steered Patrick toward the freezers. "Hey, there, Mr. Chin," she called to the small man behind the counter.

Soon they were back outside sliding the wrappers off two ice cream bars. But before Patrick could take a bite, a voice stopped him cold.

"Well, look at this. Eskimo Pies. Wasn't I just saying I wanted an Eskimo Pie, Danny?"

Patrick and Nairen wheeled around to face the voice. Two boys, one twice the size of the other, leaned in cool comfort against the store. The bigger boy peeled himself away from the wall and strolled threateningly toward them.

"Who's this?" he asked, planting himself inches away from Patrick.

Nairen cleared her throat uneasily. "Marion Trent. Danny Plato. Meet Patrick Meeres. Patrick's dad is our new principal."

Marion raised an eyebrow. "Hey, Danny, get over here and meet the principal's kid."

The smaller boy scurried toward them. He looked like a pint-sized hood. In spite of the summer heat, he wore a black leather jacket and his hair was greased back in a ducktail.

"Welcome to Waskasoo City, Fatso," Danny said.

"Thanks loads, Shrimp." Patrick regretted the words even before they'd left his mouth.

"Watch it, Lard Butt." Danny rushed forward and shoved Patrick hard in the chest.

"Shrimp," Marion said to himself and laughed. "I think you're in trouble, Danny. Nicknames like that have a way of sticking to a guy."

Danny's face blazed. He balled up his fist and started for Patrick. Suddenly, the ground rocked. Like the deck of a ship, it rolled beneath them for several seconds while the din of shattering glass cut through the air.

Chapter Two

Danny fell to a crouching position, his head turning wildly from side to side. A wail rose from inside The Corner Store, and everyone turned toward the sound.

"A whole shelf of dill pickles," cried Mr. Chin. The smell of spiced vinegar wafted through the screen doors and over the sidewalk.

"Come on, Danny. Let's go," said Marion, his eyes wide.

"What happened, Marion? What . . ."

"Let's go, I said," Marion snapped. "Oh, and we'll take those Eskimo Pies, young ladies." He plucked the ice cream deftly from Patrick and Nairen, and then the two quickly rounded the side of the store and disappeared.

Patrick wanted to be angry, to defend himself and Nairen. Instead, his stomach flip-flopped in sudden relief.

"The big creep." Nairen clenched her fists angrily.

"Don't you mean *little* creep?" asked Patrick, his voice quavering.

"I'm talking about Marion. He bullies everybody at Craven Hill. Sometimes he uses Danny to do his dirty work because he thinks it's funny. A name like Marion just makes him meaner. Last year a new kid called him Maid Marion behind his back. That kid ended up with two black eyes and a bloody nose. He was too afraid to tell who beat him up. But everyone knew."

"Wow," Patrick whispered, glancing nervously over his shoulder. Looking back at Nairen he asked, "Was that an earthquake?"

"I didn't think Waskasoo City had earthquakes. But what else could it've been?" Then Nairen laughed. "Danny looked ready to wet his pants."

Patrick didn't smile. "Whatever it was, I think it saved my skin . . . my *fat* skin."

"Don't take Danny seriously," Nairen said. "You're not all that fat."

"Thanks a million," Patrick muttered, throwing Nairen a dirty look.

"No, I didn't mean that the way it sounded. I meant . . ." She shrugged awkwardly, looking down at her tall, thin legs. "Danny calls me Stork Girl sometimes. Just don't pay attention. Come on, I'll show you the library."

Patrick nodded glumly. He'd seen enough of Waskasoo City and had enough of making friends for one day. But he needed books, so he followed Nairen down the street.

Nairen hadn't told Patrick that the library was fifteen blocks from The Corner

Store, so he felt even grumpier by the time they arrived. In spite of this, he was drawn to the ivy-draped building the moment he saw it and liked the inside even better. "More books than New Castle's library," he said, his eyes burning eagerly.

He asked for a library card, discovered that he could check out as many books as he wanted, and then spent an hour rifling through the shelves while Nairen read magazines. In the end, he checked out four Agatha Christie mysteries, a new award winner from the children's section called *Rifles for Watie,* and several oversize books about dinosaurs.

"Hey, we've got to carry these a long way. Did you have to check out the whole library?" Nairen complained. "Those dinosaur books are the size of a tyrannosaurus rex."

"Mind your own business," Patrick snapped. "You dragged me clear across town, so let me get what I want."

"What's with you?" Nairen turned and marched out the library door.

Patrick followed, struggling with his stack of books, and found her sitting on the curb. "Sorry," he mumbled to the back of her head. "I'm just tired, I guess."

"Yeah, well take it out on someone else," she said, without turning around.

"I will. Any little kids in the neighborhood? Skinny kids I could sit on?"

Nairen laughed. "Yeah, Petey James—the meanest kid on the planet. He flattened all four tires on dad's car last month. All four!" She stood and took *Rifles for Watie* and the Agatha Christie mysteries from Patrick. "Now I ask you, where did a four-year-old learn how to do that?"

Nairen talked and smiled nonstop all the way home, which Patrick took as a sign that she'd forgiven him. By the time they reached their block, the moving van was gone, and Patrick wanted to hurry home to check out his new room. Before he left,

Nairen suggested catching the Saturday matinee at the Paramount. Patrick found he couldn't say no, not after the way he'd acted. But when he thought about it later, he was really glad she'd asked.

Patrick's room was wall-to-wall boxes. Instead of working on the mess, he dumped the library books and curled up in the only empty space to finish his ghost story. Suddenly, his father appeared at the door.

"I need your help unpacking."

"I want to finish my book," Patrick answered.

"Oh, come on! You think I can do all this by myself?"

"It wasn't my idea to move," Patrick muttered.

"Get in here now," Mr. Meeres ordered, his voice stony.

After two silent hours of sorting and arranging their belongings, Mr. Meeres stood up straight, kneading his back muscles with his fingers. It was well past supper time. "We're eating out," he said, surveying the tumble of boxes.

In a few minutes, their car rolled into the parking lot of a drive-in restaurant. The carhop couldn't stop talking about the earthquake, hardly giving them a chance to order. But when she was finally gone, they sat in uncomfortable silence.

At last, Mr. Meeres cleared his throat. "Did you feel the earthquake?" he asked.

Patrick nodded.

"When the floor started shaking, I figured the movers had backed their truck into the house." Mr. Meeres stared blankly out the windshield. "Did you like Nairen?" he asked absently.

"She's okay," said Patrick.

"You're making this rough on me, buddy." Mr. Meeres's voice was tired.

"We're going to the movies tomorrow afternoon."

"You are?" Michael Meeres smiled faintly. "That's good."

It turned out to be a very late supper. The sun was already sliding out of sight as Patrick and his father left the drive-in. Instead of heading home, Mr. Meeres guided the car toward Craven Hill School to pick up an enrollment list.

Patrick had seen Craven Hill before, when they had come to town to look for a house, but that had been in the daylight. Suddenly the massive structure loomed above the trees, and Patrick was surprised at how different—how sinister—it looked in the gathering dusk. *Like Dracula's castle,* he thought.

A tall estate fence, built of brick pillars and sharp iron rods, circled the school. Great blocks of stone formed the foundation and dark bricks rose three stories and beyond to form several pointed towers. A belfry straddled the gabled roof, and in the last throes of light, Patrick thought he could see dark, winged shapes bobbing and weaving in the air around it.

"Bats," said his father, pointing to the sky. "Gives the place character."

They parked along the street, then walked through an arched gateway—the rear entrance to the school grounds—and down a wide stone path lined with oak trees. The walkway divided, leading to the east and the west doors of the school. Mr. Meeres followed the west fork.

"Why'd this town build a castle for a school?" asked Patrick, as he felt his way in the dark. There were no lights along the path, and the darkness made him feel strangely afraid. He found comfort in the sound of his own voice.

"They didn't," Mr. Meeres answered out of the blackness. "Some rich English immigrant—a fellow named Paginet—had it built for the children of Waskasoo."

"He just *gave* it to the city?"

"That's right. He sailed back to England when World War I started, but he left an endowment that still keeps the school library staffed and supplied. I guess the old fellow loved books."

As they rounded the building, their way was suddenly lit by an ornate light fixture hanging above two stout wooden doors. A substantial set of stone steps led to the doors, above which the word GIRLS was sculpted into the curved stone lintel.

"The girls' entrance," Mr. Meeres explained. "There's an identical set of steps and doors on the other side for boys. Up until this year, the school board kept girls and boys separated during recess. But I insisted that we stop living in the dark ages."

Mr. Meeres fumbled with his keys, finally unlocking the massive doors. They passed through a vestibule and a second set of doors into the foyer. On one side, a sweeping wooden staircase wound to the upper stories. Directly across the foyer, Patrick saw the boys' entrance. Single lamps in each vestibule shone through the glass door panels, providing the only light in the building. A dark hallway opposite the staircase led past the classroom doors. The principal's office was at the far end.

Not bothering to find the light switch, Mr. Meeres marched down the hall with Patrick in tow. His leather shoes rapped on the hardwood floor, echoing eerily from the stairs behind them. When they reached the end of the hall, Mr. Meeres fumbled with his keys again, finally finding the lock and opening his office. He flipped on the lights, blinding Patrick momentarily, and made his way quickly to a large oak desk.

"Where did I leave that list?" he asked, turning to a file cabinet and poking about inside.

Patrick wandered back into the hall and peered past the jet-black classrooms to the dimly lit foyer. The wide staircase with its heavy oak banisters caught his attention, and a sudden, unexplainable spike of fear stabbed his heart. Yet he felt drawn toward the stairs and began to move silently, on tiptoes, down the dark expanse of hallway.

Chapter Three

When he reached the foot of the staircase, Patrick stood and stared up at the landing, where the stairway split, marching upward to the left and to the right. Tall windows, each crowned with an arch of stained glass, lined the landing. He started up the wooden stairs, still walking on tiptoes.

He paused on the landing and turned to look at the splash of light from his father's office that washed across the polished floor. But the office seemed far away to Patrick—a blip of light on the horizon. He turned back to the stairway, feeling oddly sluggish and disoriented. Slowly, Patrick climbed the flight of stairs to his left. The light from the foyer faded quickly, and Patrick gripped the banister as he reached blindly with his toes for each step. He came to another, smaller landing where the stairs turned back on themselves and headed to the second floor foyer. As if in a dream, Patrick felt his way to the top.

He shuffled to the center of the foyer. Behind him the stairs continued to the third level. His eyes strained against the blackness of another hallway. Patrick shivered, despite the warm summer night, as an icy wind swirled about his ankles, and then disappeared. He sensed the wintery draft whirling away down the hall. Icy fingers tugged at his thoughts, urging him to follow. He took several faltering steps into the inky cavern.

Somewhere along the hallway, a pinpoint of light caught his eye. It flickered near one of the classroom doors, then began to grow rapidly. The light strengthened until an object within it took on a distinct shape.

Terror shot through Patrick's body. His throat closed, and he tried to run. But his legs wouldn't respond. Quaking, he stood bathed in the soft, blue-green glow of a small human figure.

A little boy, no older than seven or eight, floated to the arched entrance of what was clearly the library, now visible in the ghostly light. The boy stood still for a moment, then turned a pallid face toward Patrick—a face so wrenched with anger and despair that Patrick flinched under its piercing stare. Dark, hollow eyes held him in their crushing grip until he thought his brain would burst. Then, the tiny figure turned away, releasing Patrick, who tumbled to the floor.

The boy floated to the library doors and passed easily through the solid wood and glass, leaving a terrifying blackness behind.

Patrick scrambled to his feet and ran pell-mell for the stairs.

"Dad! Dad!"

Mr. Meeres was already running from his office. He grabbed his son's shoulders, shaking him. "Patrick, settle down. What's going on?"

"Up there!" Patrick waved his arm frantically, pointing to the stairs. "There's someone up there! On the second floor!"

"What! Who's up there?"

"A boy. I saw a little boy. He walked into the library. Right through the door, Dad. He glowed blue. No, green . . ."

"Hold on. You're babbling, Patrick. Maybe you saw your own reflection in one of the glass door panels. I scared myself silly that way once, when I was about your age."

"But Dad, he was small. Maybe seven. And blue-green."

Mr. Meeres's brow furrowed. "Well, I suppose some kids might have broken into the school. Come on, we'll check. What were you doing up there, anyway?"

Patrick shrugged and reluctantly followed his father back up the stairs. Mr. Meeres felt around for the light switch.

"There," said his father, as the hallway suddenly sprang out of the darkness. "Now, let's find your little culprit."

Mr. Meeres rattled every door up and down the hall, including the double doors leading into the library. They were all locked.

"No one could have gone into the library without a key, Patrick." Mr. Meeres tried a few of his keys until the library opened. He flipped on the lights, and they stood in the doorway surveying the empty tables and chairs.

"Just to be sure, we'll check all the nooks and crannies," said Mr. Meeres.

Long rows of thick, floor-to-ceiling bookshelves built of fine-grained oak lined the library. Patrick and his father checked every aisle between the shelves, looked under every desk and table, and tried the storage areas to make sure they were locked. But Patrick stopped short near a large map cabinet. An icy wind swirled around his legs and was gone before he could cry out. Clearly, his father had felt nothing, so Patrick choked back his fear.

Mr. Meeres locked the library and led Patrick upstairs to the third floor, which was mostly a large open area used as a recreation hall. They checked the doors and windows.

"These fire escape doors have crash bars. I suppose someone could have gone out this way. If he did, he can't get back in," said Mr. Meeres. "That's enough of this. Let's go home."

"But Dad, I really saw something. And it wasn't my reflection. Honest. You've got to believe me," Patrick begged.

"That's enough," snapped Mr. Meeres. "We checked the whole place. Give it up." He stomped toward the stairs.

"You never listen! You haven't listened since Mom died, and you're even worse now that we're living here. What I say never counts for anything!"

Mr. Meeres whirled around. "Oh, I get it. This is about leaving New Castle, isn't it?"

Patrick didn't answer.

"Isn't it!" his father shouted.

Patrick's legs were shaky, but he pushed past his father and wobbled down the stairs. Back in the office, standing in the bright lights, he began to wonder if he'd been imagining things.

"Patrick?" Mr. Meeres stood in the office doorway. "I'm sorry."

Patrick nodded curtly and turned away.

They left the school through the girls' entrance, Mr. Meeres carefully securing the door behind them. In minutes they were home, and Patrick wasted no time in going to bed.

Lying in the dark, Patrick felt the room's emptiness. His room in New Castle had always felt so inviting, as if he belonged there, but he'd gladly settle for this emptiness if it meant no icy breezes or strange little boys.

How long Patrick slept, he didn't know. Suddenly, he was wide awake, searching the silent darkness. He glanced at the lighted dial of his alarm clock. It was midnight. A mournful sound echoed through the deserted streets and into his window—the tolling of a bell. Without ever having heard it, Patrick knew it was the bell in Craven Hill's tower. One deep, mellow, lonely knell.

Chapter Four

"Move it to the right just a tad. A little more. Good. Hold it right there." Mr. Meeres hurried forward to mark the spot where Patrick held up a gold-framed seascape.

Stifling a yawn, Patrick lowered the painting and stood back while his father tapped a nail into the wall.

"Trouble sleeping?" asked Mr. Meeres.

"The bell woke me up." Patrick yawned again. "Couldn't go back to sleep." He'd lain frozen in his bed for hours, afraid of what might be waiting at his window.

"Bell?" asked Patrick's father.

"The school bell." Patrick hesitated. "It rang once. At midnight."

Mr. Meeres grabbed the seascape and hung it on the nail. He stepped back to see if it was level, then turned to Patrick. "No one was in the school last night, Patrick," he said. "No one."

"I heard the bell! Just because you were asleep . . ." Patrick bit back his words and headed to his room. His father didn't stop him.

Patrick put away the rest of his things and hung his pterodactyl model from the ceiling. He worked quickly, energized by both his anger and a strange sense of foreboding. Then he threw himself on his bed and watched the pterodactyl spin lazily on its string.

He heard his father angrily tearing through boxes in the living room and tried to block out the sound with one of the dinosaur books. It was no use. He couldn't concentrate. He wondered miserably if he was crazy—hearing bells, seeing blue-green boys.

His father rapped once on Patrick's door and came in right away.

"I phoned the Parks Department, and I think I can get you a spot in the summer softball league," he said, trying to smile. "Even though they've been playing for several weeks. How about it?"

Patrick shook his head.

"Reggie had talked you into playing back in New Castle. Come on, you need the exercise."

"Next year, Dad," Patrick said, without looking up. "I'll do it next summer, okay?"

Mr. Meeres turned to leave. He stopped and said over his shoulder. "Maybe there was another tremor last night. Could've rung the bell."

"Maybe," said Patrick.

His father stared at him for a moment, then quietly closed the door.

An hour later, Patrick wandered over to the Potters' house. Nairen was sitting on her front steps watching Marla spin her Hula-Hoop. She smiled and waved when Patrick appeared.

"A-thousand fifty . . . a-thousand fifty-one . . . a-thousand fifty-two," droned Marla.

"She's going for the world record." Nairen groaned. "No one seems to know what the record is, so Marla decided she'd go so high it'd have to be a record. Let's get out of here before I go nutty. Donnie said he'd drop us off at the movies. Hey, Donnie," she called over her shoulder. "Patrick's here. Let's go."

"Donnie?"

"He's my older brother. He's seventeen and has his own car."

An even taller version of Marla, but with a crew cut, pushed open the screen door. "Hi," said Donnie, nodding to Patrick. "Climb in." He pointed proudly to an old, but newly painted Studebaker sitting in the driveway.

Nairen jabbered all the way to town, while Donnie revved his engine and honked at people he knew. But Patrick wasn't listening to Nairen or paying attention to Donnie. His mind had wandered back to Craven Hill School.

"Thanks, Donnie," Nairen said, and Patrick realized that the car had rolled to a stop. After they slid out, Donnie gave them a little salute and laid rubber pulling away from the curb.

Patrick and Nairen paid for their tickets and walked down the red carpeted steps to the Paramount's lobby. At the snack bar, they each bought a large Coke and a bag of popcorn, then went to find some good seats.

"How about the balcony?" said Patrick. But when they reached the foot of the stairs, they bumped into Marion and Danny.

"Hey, it's Lard Butt," sneered Danny, blocking the stairs.

"Out of the way," said Nairen.

Marion laughed, then turned his eyes on Patrick. "I'm starting to wonder about you. I never see you with any guys. You and Nairen play house this morning?"

"That's enough, Pea Brain," growled Nairen. "Now get out of the way."

Marion snagged Nairen's ponytail and twisted, pulling her head close to his face.

"Listen, Stretch, I'm not a pea brain. Got that?"

An usher started toward them. Marion dropped Nairen's ponytail and took the balcony stairs two at a time. Danny had already disappeared.

Nairen waved the usher away. "It's okay," she said, trying to smile.

Patrick leaned against the wall to support his wobbly legs, but Nairen grabbed his arm and pulled him toward the lower level seats.

"I like the back of the theater," she said, as if nothing was wrong. "How about you?"

"Me, too," Patrick agreed, keeping his voice level. He turned his head so Nairen couldn't see his face burning with shame.

"This is a great movie," said Nairen as they sat down and waited for the lights to dim.

The feature was an old favorite, *Abbott and Costello Meet Frankenstein*. Patrick had seen it twice before and was always ready to see it again. As far as he was concerned, no one was funnier than Lou Costello.

Suddenly Nairen jumped out of her seat. "Oh, yuck!" she yelled, brushing frantically at her lap.

Patrick looked over, mystified. Something wet dribbled into his lap, as harsh laughter broke out from above. Marion and Danny were leaning over the balcony railing.

"Looks like you need your diaper changed, Fatso," Danny jeered, an empty cup still in his hand. "You, too, Stork Girl."

"You creeps!" Nairen spat the words through clenched teeth.

"Hey, settle down, Potter." Marion smiled benevolently. "It was an accident, wasn't it, Danny?"

"Pure accident," Danny agreed. "Didn't even know you were down there, Porky."

"Just to show you how sorry we are, take my Coke," Marion said as he casually reached over the railing and dropped his cup. Before Patrick and Nairen could escape, they were doused with soda.

Just then a giant hand clamped onto Marion's shoulder. The usher's other hand held the collar of Danny's leather jacket. "That's it for you," he said, shaking Danny like a rag doll. "Throwing stuff off the balcony is a one-way ticket out of here."

As the usher hauled the two boys away,

Marion turned a steely eye on Patrick. Then he smiled cheerfully.

Everyone else in the theater had their eyes on Patrick and Nairen, who hurried out to the rest rooms to clean up. By the time they got back to their seats, the lights had dimmed and the newsreel was beginning.

"That was embarrassing," Nairen whispered, then fell into an angry silence that lasted through the newsreel, the Buck Rogers serial, and the Bugs Bunny cartoon.

Patrick didn't feel like talking anyway and was lost in his own thoughts. But the antics of Abbott and Costello soon revived both their spirits. Patrick was having a great time watching brainless Wilbur, Lou Costello's character, talking on the phone long distance to the Wolfman. Then Nairen leaned over and whispered in his ear.

"Wilbur's stupid, but he's a rocket scientist compared to Maid Marion and Danny."

Patrick laughed, though he wished she hadn't reminded him of Marion Trent.

Danny's loud mouth didn't scare him nearly as much as Marion's smile.

Before long, they reached one of Patrick's favorite scenes. Abbott and Costello were unpacking two crates at McDougal's House of Horrors during a terrible thunderstorm. They still didn't know that Dracula and Frankenstein were in the boxes until poor Wilbur unpacked Dracula's coffin. He tried again and again to convince his friend, Chick, that the Prince of Darkness was raising and lowering the lid. Of course, Dracula never opened the coffin when Chick was around.

"This is great," Nairen whispered and then sputtered with laughter as Wilbur tried calling Chick for help. He was so frightened he'd lost his voice.

Finally, with Chick out of the room, Dracula rose from his coffin. Staring deeply into Wilbur's eyes and waving his fingers hypnotically, the Count soon had him in a trance.

Patrick smiled as this sequence began, but the smile quickly became an expression of horror. A figure had stepped from the shadows behind Dracula and Wilbur, a small figure radiating blue-green light from the midst of the black-and-white film.

He recognized the face immediately, but for the first time Patrick noticed the boy was dressed in knickers, a white shirt with a sailor's collar, and heavy, high-topped leather shoes. Old-fashioned clothes that didn't fit with the movie.

Patrick felt as if his lungs had collapsed. He gulped for air as the boy stared deeply into his eyes. But this time the specter did not remain silent. Its grim slit of a mouth spoke a single word:

Patrick.

Chapter Five

Patrick's mouth opened in a silent scream. Falling across Nairen's legs, he bolted for the lobby. Nairen found him leaning over the water fountain, his forehead against the cool porcelain.

"Are you sick?" she asked. "Are you going to throw up?"

Patrick shook his head.

"Well, what's wrong? You scared me to death."

"I can't tell you." Patrick glanced up at her.

"You look like you've just seen a ghost. Maybe I'd better get you home."

"I'm not sick."

"Was it the popcorn? Mine seemed okay."

"Nairen, I'm not sick," Patrick said louder. "I just can't go back in there. I'll wait for you out here."

"Hey, what's going on? Come on, tell me." Nairen put her fists on her hips and glared at Patrick. When he didn't answer, she said, "Look, I still think you're sick. Come on, I'm taking you home."

Patrick allowed Nairen to lead him out of the theater, but when she started toward home, he dug in his heels. "Nairen, I'm not sick. Honest. I saw something that . . ."

Nairen stopped, waiting for Patrick to finish.

Patrick shrugged helplessly. "I saw something that scared me."

"What are you talking about? *Abbott and Costello Meet Frankenstein* is a comedy."

"No, you don't understand . . ."

"No, I don't," Nairen complained. "You're not making sense. Not a bit of sense. In fact, you're spooky, Patrick Meeres. You yell at me over library books. Now you run out of a funny movie because you're scared. Spooky, that's what you are."

"Oh, yeah? Just leave me alone," said Patrick, his voice strained. "I can find my own way home."

"Have it your way." Nairen started back into the theater.

"No, wait." Patrick licked his lips as Nairen turned to face him. "I've got to tell someone. But not here."

Nairen gave Patrick a long, hard look, then grabbed his arm and pulled him down the street. She pushed him into the Sweete Shoppe and guided him into a booth. They ordered milk shakes, and Patrick waited until their order came before saying anything.

Loud music from the jukebox covered their conversation, giving Patrick the privacy he needed. With Elvis Presley singing in the background, he forced himself to tell Nairen about last night's encounter with the phantom child. Her mouth opened and closed, and her eyes widened. Twice she whistled softly, but Patrick was sure she didn't believe him. Until he told her about the bell.

Nairen sat up straight, a faraway look in her eyes. "I heard the bell, Patrick. I woke up just before it rang. The sound made me feel . . . empty inside, and lonely. And cold. And afraid. I had trouble going back to sleep." Her eyes suddenly focused, and she looked at Patrick. "I asked mom and dad about the bell. No one else in our family heard it. They thought I was dreaming."

"I know the feeling," said Patrick.

"But what does this have to do with the movie?" asked Nairen.

Patrick hesitated. "I saw the kid again," he said slowly, then rushed ahead. "Right there in the middle of the screen, standing between Dracula and Lou Costello. He was shining blue-green, and he was wearing knickers and old-fashioned shoes. It sounds crazy, Nairen, but he was there." Patrick searched Nairen's face but couldn't tell what she was thinking.

"I didn't see him," said Nairen. "Are you sure?"

"Nairen, he said my name. He looked right at me, and said, 'Patrick.'"

"You heard him?"

"Yes." Patrick cradled his head in his hands. "I wouldn't believe me, either."

"I didn't say I didn't believe you, Patrick." Nairen reached out and touched his arm. "I admit I probably wouldn't have, if it weren't for the bell. The sound of the bell . . ."

Patrick looked up from the table. Nairen's eyes had the faraway look again.

"When I heard the bell, it's like I knew something weird was going to happen." Nairen smiled, the spell broken. "Hey, if the Russians can send a dog into space, why can't there be ghosts?"

Patrick felt a rush of relief pinken his cheeks. He could have hugged her. "Thank you," he said. "Thank you, thank you, thank you."

Nairen waved off his gratitude. She seemed excited now. "This is like a story from *Web of Mystery*, Patrick. So, what happens next?"

"Wait and see, I guess. This kid isn't through with me, though. And neither are Marion and Danny. Isn't life great?"

They left the malt shop and walked home along the old railroad spur. The towers of Craven Hill School were visible in the distance, and Patrick stopped to stare at them. *Who are you?* he thought as he gazed at the building. *And what do you want from me?*

When they reached Nairen's house, they found Mrs. Potter at the kitchen table hunched over a paint-by-numbers project.

"It's a mystery canvas. Don't know what you've got until you're done," explained Nairen's mother. "You must be Patrick." She extended a paint-stained hand.

Patrick shook hands, then he and Nairen peered over Mrs. Potter's shoulder. The painting *was* a mystery. The maze of light blue lines twisted and turned on one another, making such tiny shapes that the numbers barely fit inside. Though Mrs. Potter had colored a third of the painting, the subject was still a puzzle.

"Well, enough of this for today," said Mrs. Potter, as she stood and started clearing the table. "By the way, our little Hula-Hooper pooped out at twenty-five hundred. Pretty good, don't you think?"

"Amazing," said Patrick, and really meant it.

"Now that mom's moved her paints, how about a game of Scrabble?" Nairen suggested.

Patrick loved Scrabble, so they got out the board while Mrs. Potter cleaned her paintbrushes. They had played for about thirty minutes when the doorbell rang.

"Patrick," Mrs. Potter called from the front room. "Your father's here."

"What does he want?" Patrick muttered.

When they reached the living room, Mr. Meeres was just settling onto the sofa. "Hi, kids. When you weren't home, Patrick, I figured you'd be here. How was the movie?"

Nairen caught Patrick's eye. "Abbott and Costello are always funny," she answered.

"No one funnier," Patrick's father agreed. "Say, I'm here to offer both of you jobs. The school librarian called this afternoon."

"Mrs. Stanier?" asked Nairen.

Mr. Meeres nodded. "She's facing a mountain of work in the library, more than she can handle, and she needs to get it done before school starts. She asked for help, and I suggested you two. What do you think?"

"What exactly would we be doing?" asked Patrick.

"Oh, moving books, gluing in book pockets. Things like that. The school can't pay big wages, say forty cents a hour, but I'll try to make it up to you somehow."

Patrick and Nairen exchanged glances.

"Sure, Mr. Meeres," said Nairen. "Thanks. When do we start?"

"She wants you there early Monday morning. You can catch a ride with me at eight."

After a few more minutes visiting Mrs. Potter, Mr. Meeres left for home, and Patrick and Nairen headed back to the kitchen.

"I could use a little extra money," said Nairen. "That was nice of your dad."

"He's just trying to keep me busy so I won't miss . . ." A loud racket, like hail bouncing off a tin roof, exploded from the kitchen.

"The Scrabble board," yelled Nairen. "Marla!"

They ran into the kitchen, but nobody was there. Scrabble tiles were scattered across the floor, and the box had been tossed in the corner by the refrigerator. The board was still in the middle of the table, though most of the tiles had been stripped from its surface.

Patrick and Nairen approached the table. In the middle of the board carefully arranged letters spelled out the words, *HELP ME HELP BAR.* Six other tiles lay randomly on the board as if someone had planned to use them, too: N, blank, E, Y, A, T.

"How . . . Patrick, no one had time to do this and get out of the kitchen." Nairen stood looking dumbfounded at the Scrabble board and then at the tiles on the floor.

Patrick began to tremble. "What's this mean, Nairen? Who needs help?"

That night, at midnight, the bell at Craven Hill School tolled again—a single, dreadful stroke.

Chapter Six

Patrick didn't see Nairen on Sunday. Her family went to church that morning and then visited her grandparents several miles away in Sylvan City.

After lunch, Mr. Meeres coaxed Patrick into the car, and they toured the surrounding countryside. On the northeastern edge of town, they discovered the Gaetz Memorial Bird Sanctuary, a tract of forest preserve donated by one of Waskasoo City's early settlers.

They parked the car and walked the shaded trails, listening for birds and watching squirrels play in the branches overhead. Patrick had never been in such a peaceful place. One trail led past a pond and deeper into the woods until it ended abruptly at the edge of a steep cliff.

"Would you look at that?" said Mr. Meeres. After the cool, green light of the forest, the bright sunlight forced him to shade his eyes as he peered over the cliff. "It's the Waskasoo River."

Patrick leaned on the metal rail that protected hikers from falling. As he gazed at the dark water far below, a cold hand wrapped its fingers around his bare arm. Patrick spun around, but no one was there. He jumped back from the edge as the icy touch spread through his torso and out to his fingers and toes. Then his nostrils filled with a damp, moldy smell mingled with the stench of rotting flesh. He gagged.

Mr. Meeres had wandered down the trail, along the brink of the cliff. Patrick tried yelling to his father but couldn't catch his breath. Just when he thought he might vomit, the cold hand lifted and the foul odors drifted away. He leaned against the rail, gasping.

"Hey, Patrick," Mr. Meeres called. "Are you ready to head back to the car?"

Patrick managed a brief wave that his father took as a "yes." By the time Mr. Meeres reached him, Patrick was breathing normally again. Judging from his father's smile, it was obvious that he hadn't felt or smelled anything out of the ordinary.

During the remainder of their drive, Patrick huddled silently on the car seat. The hot July sun seeped slowly into his bones, pushing away the cold, while Mr. Meeres chattered happily about the bird sanctuary, his new job, and how much he liked Waska-soo City. Patrick hardly heard a word.

To his surprise, Patrick slept soundly that night—so soundly that if the bell at

Craven Hill rang, he didn't hear it. He was exhausted by the events of the past three days, and sleep was a welcome escape. Patrick dreamed that his mother came to his bedside, her light touch brushing his forehead. But as soon as he awoke, chilling memories of the bird sanctuary drove anything pleasant from his mind.

Patrick wanted desperately to tell Nairen about the icy hand, but Mrs. Stanier kept them so busy on Monday morning that finding a private moment was impossible. She put each of them to work in a different part of the library, shifting books from shelf to shelf.

In the morning sunlight, the old library was warm and friendly, completely different from the terrifying place of two nights ago. But this was where the boy in the knickers first appeared, and Patrick was certain that the library was at the center of the mystery.

At noon, Patrick and Nairen were happy to escape all the lifting and toting. They grabbed their lunch sacks and headed for the school yard, running out the boys' entrance and over to a park bench resting in the shade of a huge oak.

"Hey," said Patrick, as they wolfed down their food. "What's that?" He pointed to a green steel tube that stood against the old school building and extended from the ground to the top floor.

"A fire escape," Nairen said. "A really great fire escape. There's a slide inside that twists around and down."

Patrick's eyes lit up. "I wonder if dad would let us give it a try?"

"Well, if the past is any judge, I'd say there isn't a chance," said Nairen. "Last year, some kids found the bottom door of the tube unlocked. They spent most of their lunch hour running up to the third floor and then sliding down—until our old principal caught them. You'd have thought they'd robbed a bank, the way he carried on. No,

Patrick, 'doing the tube' for fun is a felony in Waskasoo School District."

Patrick looked longingly at the tall green fire escape, standing like a rocket ship on its launching pad. "You're probably right. My dad usually sticks to the rules." Patrick paused, his eyes suddenly darkening. "Nairen, have you been to the bird sanctuary?"

"Sure. We used to go there for field trips. Why?"

Patrick remembered the cold touch and shivered. He stared at the blank windows of the school, then turned hollow eyes toward Nairen and sighed. Slowly, he told her about Sunday.

"This is too weird." Nairen jumped up and circled the bench. "Do you think the cold, stinky hand belongs to the kid in the knickers?"

"I suppose so."

"I heard the bell again Saturday night. Did you hear it?"

Patrick nodded.

"What's it mean?" asked Nairen. "Any ideas?"

Patrick didn't answer. Instead, he stood and walked toward the fire escape. Nairen followed close behind. When he reached the tube, Patrick placed both hands flat against the sun-warmed metal.

"I don't know what it means," he said, at last. "I just know I want it to stop."

"Well, I have an idea. I think you're being called by the other side," said Nairen. "Called to help a restless spirit. And once you help, he— it—will leave you alone."

Patrick turned to Nairen. "Oh? And how did you figure this out?"

"The Scrabble board."

"Just because 'help' was spelled out doesn't mean I've been 'called' to do the helping."

"Could be exactly what it means. Did you think about adding the extra letters to the message, Patrick? Well, did you?"

"No." Patrick looked puzzled.

"Well, I did. Those extra letter tiles weren't left on the board by accident, you know. I think we interrupted whatever . . . whoever left the message. So, I played around with the letters to see what other words I could make."

"I don't even remember what the other letters were," said Patrick.

"*N, E, Y, A, T*, and a blank." Nairen rolled her eyes in disbelief. "How could you forget? Anyhow, I wondered about the blank first. Of course, the blank could stand for anything, but I figured it had to represent a letter that there weren't enough tiles for in the Scrabble set. Sure enough, there are only two *H* and two *P* tiles, and *HELP ME HELP BAR* uses all of them. So, the blank stands for either *P* or *H* because no other letter was used up.

"So, I asked myself what words I could make with *N, E, Y, A, T*, and *P* or *H*. I came up with weird stuff like 'pay net' or 'hay net' or 'hey nat' or 'yap net' or 'they tan.' But none of them fit: *HELP ME HELP BAR THEY TAN.*"

Patrick smiled.

"Next I tried adding on to the last word, *BAR.* I came up with *BARE PANTY.*"

This time Patrick laughed.

"Then I came up with a few other stupid choices, like *BARN PEATY* or *BARNY PEAT.* But then *BARNY PEAT* suddenly seemed to mean something, and with a little rearranging I got *BARNEY PAT.*" Nairen looked smug.

"So?" said Patrick.

"No commas in Scrabble!" cried Nairen. "Don't you see? The message is to you: *HELP ME. HELP BARNEY, PAT.* After all that's happened to you, this shouldn't be a surprise. Barney needs your help, Pat."

"Who's Barney?" Patrick asked. "The kid in the knickers?"

Nairen shrugged. "Hey, maybe I put a period where it doesn't belong. Maybe the message says *HELP ME HELP BARNEY.* You know, the spirit wants you to help him help this Barney guy."

"You know any Barneys living around here?"

"No, but we could ask around. Find a Barney in some sort of trouble."

"What if the cold hands belong to a different ghost," Patrick suggested. "Maybe he's Barney."

"Let's ask Mrs. Stanier."

Patrick gaped at Nairen. "You're nuts! 'Ah, Mrs. Stanier, about this ghost I've been having trouble with . . .'"

"No, I mean let's ask her some questions about the school. Mrs. Stanier went to Craven Hill when she was a kid. Maybe she knows something that could give us a clue."

"Like what?"

"Oh, I don't know. Maybe something awful happened in the school way back when. Like somebody got killed. Aren't ghosts supposed to be the unsettled spirits of people who died violent deaths or lived unhappy lives? And isn't the school where all the haunting started?"

Before Patrick could answer, a loud twang caused both of them to flinch. A rock ricocheted off the tube and clattered against the stone foundation.

"Not a bad throw, right, Patty?" Marion smirked from his perch atop one of the brick pillars of the school's fence.

Danny popped out from behind the pillar. "Marion's got a great pitching arm. Better watch your rear end, Lard Butt."

Marion wound up and let another rock fly. Patrick and Nairen jumped behind the tube as it slammed into the metal exactly where Patrick had been standing.

"Steee-rike two," Danny shrieked.

"It's safe now, Patty. I'm out of rocks," Marion called.

"The name's Patrick," Patrick shouted as he stepped out into view.

"Oh, that's right. It's Patrick." Marion slapped his forehead. "You've been hang-

ing around with Nairen so much, I got confused. So, if you're a Patrick and not a Patty,
that must mean you two are in love."

Danny laughed. Then he began to sing,
"Fatso and Stork Girl sitting in a tree,
K-I-S-S-I-N-G."

Marion motioned for Danny to be quiet.
"Don't forget, I owe you big time for getting
us kicked out of the movies." He smiled and
shook his head slowly. "I really hated missing Abbott and Costello."

Marion waved as if he were saying good-
bye to old friends and turned to jump
down from the pillar. Suddenly he wheeled
around, hurling one more rock.

Patrick was so surprised that he was slow
to retreat. The stone bounced off his foot,
and he cried out in pain. Then another
rock collided with his shoulder, and Patrick
dropped to his knees.

"Idiots!" Nairen screamed after them.
She clenched her fists, her face flaming,
and kicked the tube ferociously. "I'll fix

you, I swear! You pea-brained . . . you pea-brained jackasses!"

"Go, Nairen!" Patrick grimaced, his eyes watering as he rubbed his shoulder.

Nairen looked sheepish. "Are you okay?" she asked.

"Yeah, I'll live. Lucky he wasn't closer. Come on, let's go talk to Mrs. Stanier."

The second they walked through the library door, Mrs. Stanier had them seated around a table putting labels on books and gluing in card pockets. This time the librarian worked alongside her two helpers. Once they fell into the rhythm of their work, Nairen and Patrick began to steer the conversation away from the library.

"Who built Craven Hill, Mrs. Stanier?" asked Patrick, though he already knew the answer.

"Why, Arthur Buckley Paginet, Patrick. I'm surprised your father hasn't told you all about him. A rich Englishman, he was, and very eccentric. He loved Gothic mystery stories, and he had the school built to resemble Craven Hill Manor, a spooky place in one of his favorite books. Nobody in town complained; after all, they were getting a free school. I remember my mother telling me how secretive Mr. Paginet was about the school while it was being built. He wouldn't hire local builders. Instead he brought in a construction team from England and fenced the construction site, allowing no visitors until the building was completed."

"Sounds like Mr. Paginet was pretty weird," said Patrick.

"Weird? Well, yes, I suppose he was a bit strange," said Mrs. Stanier.

"So, Craven Hill School was modeled after some creepy old mansion." Nairen lowered her voice. "Well, it gives me goose bumps, that's for sure."

Mrs. Stanier smiled. "Yes, I've been spooked a few times myself, especially working here at night."

"I'll bet there are some stories about a spooky old place like this," said Nairen. "Like someone being murdered in the bell tower or something."

Mrs. Stanier seemed shocked by Nairen's suggestion. "Why would you think such a terrible thing?" she asked, but then she pursed her lips and looked thoughtfully into space. "You know," she said after a moment, "I do remember something quite dreadful that happened in 1920. I was only ten years old and was going to school right here at Craven Hill. Mr. Dawe was our principal back then."

Mrs. Stanier stopped again, her brow wrinkling with effort as she reached for her memories. "I remember such an uproar when Mr. Dawe's eight-year-old son disappeared from the school, late one evening while his father was working in his office. The boy had been alone in the library, reading." She stopped yet again, her eyes wandering over the shelves and the tables as if trying to determine the spot where the child had been poring over his books.

"It's the last anyone ever saw of the boy," Mrs. Stanier continued. "Oh, everyone searched for him. I remember my father helping. But he was never found." She shook her head sadly. "Poor Mr. Dawe. He'd lost his wife to an illness before coming to Waskasoo. Then he lost his only son. Mr. Dawe moved away after the school year ended."

"What was the boy's name, Mrs. Stanier?" asked Patrick, a chill settling in his stomach.

"His name? When I was small, I thought I'd never forget his name. You see, we were all so frightened that the same thing would happen to us. Let's see . . . Barnaby Dawe! That's right, little Barney Dawe."

Chapter Seven

"We've got to find out more," Patrick said. They'd finished work for the day and were wandering homeward slowly. Patrick was favoring his sore foot. "Mrs. Stanier didn't remember any of the important details."

"Well, that was a long time ago, and she was just a kid when Barney disappeared," said Nairen. "Can you believe it? Barnaby Dawe! I just shivered when Mrs. Stanier said his name. Didn't you?"

They stopped in the middle of a small traffic bridge that crossed Waskasoo Creek and leaned on the rail, watching minnows flash through the water.

"Boys wore knickers in 1920, didn't they?" asked Nairen.

"Yeah, I think so." Patrick picked up a pebble from the sidewalk and dropped it into the creek. The minnows scattered as it hit the surface.

"Well, it all matches," said Nairen. "Barney Dawe was eight years old when he disappeared from the library. You saw an eight-year-old in 1920s' clothes floating through the library door. And then there's the Scrabble message . . . No doubt about it, Barnaby Dawe is back, and he's haunting you."

Patrick picked up another pebble and tossed it out over the water in a high arc. "Let's go to the public library," he said suddenly.

"Why?"

"Old newspapers from the 1920s might tell us more about Barnaby's disappearance," said Patrick. "Give us more of the facts."

"Okay," said Nairen, "but I'm starving. Let's swing by my place for something to eat first."

Patrick and Nairen found Mrs. Potter busy at her painting, which was still pretty much of a mystery. However, when they found the cookie jar empty, they headed for Patrick's house. "I think we've got Oreos," he said.

Sure enough, Mr. Meeres had been shopping. Two packages of cookies were in the cupboard and a new bottle of milk in the fridge.

"Would your dad mind if we listened to some records?" asked Nairen, who had spotted the Meeres's record player. "You got anything good?"

"How about the Everly Brothers? *All I Have to Do Is Dream?*"

Nairen's eyes lighted up at the suggestion, so Patrick went into the living room and set up a TV tray to hold the snacks. Then he slipped the new Everly Brothers hit onto the turntable. The needle crackled momentarily as Patrick lowered the tone-arm into place.

As the song began, Nairen brought in the Oreos, then the two went back into the kitchen for glasses of milk. When they returned to the living room, the melodic sounds of the Everly Brothers washed over them. Patrick had raised the changing arm on the phonograph, which meant the record would play over and over again. Suddenly, beneath the singing voices and the guitars, they heard a strange, distorted whispering.

"What's going on?" said Patrick. "It sounded fine before."

The whispering became louder and clearer as they approached the console. A heavy coldness settled on the living room like a block of ice, and Patrick dropped his milk. The glass shattered on the floor. A hollow voice was now competing with the musicians, the words frighteningly plain: "Patrick. Help Barney. Patrick. Help Barney. Help me. Help me. Help me. Help me. . . ."

Patrick rushed forward and jerked the tonearm off the record. Nairen ran to the kitchen and came back with wet cloths to clean up the milk. Together they knelt, without speaking, picking up the broken glass and wiping the floor. Then they collapsed on the sofa, trembling in the still cold air.

Patrick glanced at Nairen, rose slowly from his seat, and inched toward the phonograph as if he were sneaking up on a dangerous animal. The turntable was still spinning, and he reached forward, setting the needle into the record grooves. The Everly Brothers sprang to life, and *All I Have to Do Is Dream* filled the room. Nairen moved to the edge of the sofa, waiting for the ghostly voice to join in with the singing. Patrick backed away from the record player, keeping what seemed to be a safe distance. They listened to the entire song. Clear, untainted Everly Brothers.

As the song ended and Patrick switched off the record player, a warm breeze blew through the room. Once again it was summer.

"I couldn't see him or hear him in the movie," Nairen said softly, "but this time I heard him plain as day. Why?"

Patrick sat down again. "I don't know," he said.

Just then the front door rattled, and Mr. Meeres strolled into the house.

"Hi, kids. I just walked over to the Potters because I thought you'd be there. Your mom sent me here, Nairen."

"We came for some Oreos," said Patrick. "Is that all right with you?"

Mr. Meeres ignored the edge in his son's voice. "Of course. But I hope you haven't spoiled your appetites. Mrs. Stanier sang your praises high and low after you left the school. She couldn't have been more pleased with your work. So, I thought I'd reward you both. Why don't we go out to a nice place for dinner? I've already cleared it with your mother, Nairen. Patrick likes Chinese, and I hear there's a great place on Gaetz Avenue, across the river."

"The Peking Duck," said Nairen. "Isn't this great, Patrick?"

Patrick frowned and swallowed his impatience. What he really wanted to do was head straight for the library.

"Let's see, it's 5:30," said Mr. Meeres. "How about we go right now?"

They loaded into the car and Mr. Meeres drove across the river bridge and up North Hill. They passed Evening Star Drive-In at the outskirts of town and pulled up in front of The Peking Duck.

The food was magnificent, so good that Patrick almost forgot about Barnaby Dawe.

Fortunately, his queasy stomach—a result of Barney's musical performance—had settled down by the time their order arrived.

After dessert, the waiter delivered the check and a small plate of fortune cookies. Mr. Meeres reached for one of the cookies and snapped it apart. "'You will change lives with your strong leadership.' Just the fortune for a school principal," he laughed.

"Mine says, 'Your natural beauty will win you approval and riches.'" Nairen snorted. "The genie of fortune cookies needs glasses."

"Not so," said Mr. Meeres. "I think his vision is quite clear. What about yours, Patrick?" his father asked.

Patrick's pleasant meal—the most enjoyable moments he'd spent with his father in days—had been suddenly ruined by the thin slip of paper in his hand. When he'd read the fortune, his heart had missed a beat.

"Same kind of junk you two got," he said, with feigned casualness. "Says I have a special talent for helping others. Can we go now?"

"Sure, I think it's time. Nairen's folks wanted her home by 8:00 to babysit Marla."

Nairen made a face. "That's right, I almost forgot. They're going to a movie."

Soon after they'd left the restaurant, the waiter began to clear the table. As he picked up the plates, his eye caught Patrick's fortune, and he stopped in surprise. It read: "Help me. Help Barney, Patrick."

Chapter Eight

"Please, Dad."

"It's nearly 7:30, Patrick. Can't it wait until tomorrow?"

"No, it can't."

Mr. Meeres sighed. "Oh, all right. It's closer to drop you off first, then take Nairen home. Does that work for you, Nairen?"

"Sure, Mr. Meeres."

Nairen shot Patrick a questioning look. He knew she wanted him to wait until she could come along.

Mr. Meeres swung the car toward town. He turned onto Ross Street and pulled over in front of the Waskasoo City Public Library.

"I'll pick you up in forty-five minutes," said Mr. Meeres, as Patrick hopped out of the car.

"I may not be ready."

"I'll be back in forty-five minutes, and that's final."

"Then I'll walk home," Patrick snapped. "Don't worry about me."

Mr. Meeres's eyes narrowed. "You're *not* walking. Be ready when I get here."

Patrick's cheeks blazed. "Then I'll call when I'm done," he said through clenched teeth.

"Listen, Patrick . . ." Mr. Meeres hesitated, then shook his head wearily. "I'll be at the school after I drop off Nairen. Try calling me there."

Patrick hurried up the steps, angry with his father for embarrassing him in front of Nairen, yet relieved that he didn't have to walk home in the dark. He hadn't wanted to argue with his father, but it was important to have enough time to find what he needed.

Patrick pushed aside his anger and embarrassment as he entered the ivy-covered library. He headed for the card catalog first and looked up nonfiction books about ghosts. One title jumped out at him, and Patrick took mental note of the call number, repeating it to himself as he searched for the right shelf.

True Appearances of the Dead—Ghosts, Hauntings, and the Supernatural World was a black, oversize volume so ancient the title had been rubbed from the spine long ago. Patrick slipped the musty-smelling book from the shelf and took it to the main desk. As the librarian was checking it out for him, Patrick asked about old copies of the Waskasoo newspaper.

"Yes," she answered, "we have back issues of the *The Waskasoo Advocate*. What dates do you need?"

Patrick remembered Mrs. Stanier saying that Barnaby Dawe disappeared in the autumn, so he requested issues published in October and November of 1920. He soon found out that *The Waskasoo Advocate* didn't become a daily newspaper until 1946—and that meant he didn't have very many papers to go through.

The old-time, small-town papers weren't hefty, so Patrick carried a thin stack to a table near the back of the library, where he was alone. Sitting near a large window overlooking a small park, Patrick began with the October issues, carefully scanning each headline.

Patrick found nothing in the October papers. He was more than halfway through November's papers, thinking that he'd have to ask the librarian for September and December, when he reached the November 20th issue. The tall, bold letters of the headline jumped out at him.

DAWE CHILD MISSING
Young Boy Kidnapped from Local School?

Waskasoo, Nov. 18—Eight-year-old Barnaby Dawe disappeared from Craven Hill School on Thursday evening, November 18. Young Barnaby accompanied his father, Craven Hill principal Abner Dawe, to the school and waited in the library while Mr. Dawe finished some paperwork in his office. When the boy's father went to retrieve his son, he discovered Barnaby was neither in the library nor anywhere in the school building. The Waskasoo City Police searched the surrounding area with no success. Volunteer search parties continue to comb the town and countryside within a several mile radius of Craven Hill School.

"We have little to go on," said Police Chief Andrew Arrington Friday afternoon, "though we have one or two individuals we are bringing in for questioning." Chief Arrington still hopes someone might come forward with information that will help solve the mystery. "Maybe someone saw or heard something unusual in the vicinity of Craven Hill School Thursday night."

Patrick's hands were shaking as he set the paper aside and reached for the issue dated November 24. Again, the lead article was about Barnaby Dawe.

SUSPECT QUESTIONED IN BARNABY DAWE DISAPPEARANCE

Former Craven Hill School Caretaker Must Answer for Suspicious Behavior

Waskasoo, Nov. 22—Terrence "Skip" Walton was detained November 22 at the Waskasoo City Police Station after being questioned about last week's disappearance of eight-year-old Barnaby Dawe from the Craven Hill School. Mr. Walton was an employee of the Waskasoo School District, assigned to Craven Hill as a custodian but released from service by Principal Abner Dawe for being intoxicated while on the job.

Mr. Walton was brought in for questioning because of an incident reported to the police on October 13. Principal Dawe summoned the city police to remove a drunken Skip Walton from the premises of Craven Hill School. Students and teachers witnessed the enraged Walton threaten Mr. Dawe. "'I'll make you pay, Abner Dawe. I will have my revenge for what you did to me.' That is what Skip Walton shouted," recalled Sarah Lassiter, third grade teacher.

Mr. Walton was released later that evening, but police warned him not to leave Waskasoo City.

Patrick still knew little more than he had learned from Mrs. Stanier, except that this

"Skip" Walton was a suspect in Barney's disappearance. Then he picked up the next issue.

SUSPECT IN BARNABY DAWE DISAPPEARANCE FALLS TO HIS DEATH

Terrence "Skip" Walton Flees Police and Plunges Over Waskasoo River Cliffs

Waskasoo, Nov. 25—It proved to be a grim Thanksgiving for Terrence "Skip" Walton and the Waskasoo City Police. Police officers were dispatched to bring in Mr. Walton of 7581 Red Deer Lane for further questioning about the abduction and possible murder of eight-year-old Barnaby Dawe, who disappeared without a trace from Craven Hill School on the evening of November 18. When officers arrived at the Walton residence at 8:15 p.m., Mr. Walton refused to open his front door and fled from the rear of his house into the Gaetz Memorial Bird Sanctuary. Police gave chase, but the wooded terrain of the sanctuary and the darkness proved to be deadly. Mr. Walton stumbled over the edge of the Waskasoo River cliffs and fell seventy feet into the shallow water near the river bank. He was pronounced dead at the scene of the accident.

Terrence Walton became the major suspect in the Dawe case after a story appeared in *The Advocate* on November 24 which reported Walton's threats against Abner Dawe, father of the missing boy, for releasing him from his custodial position at Craven Hill School. The news report prompted several people to call police headquarters to report seeing Mr. Walton at or near the Craven Hill School on the evening of November 18.

Waskasoo City Police Chief Andrew Arrington issued this statement: "We regret the death of Terrence Walton. As it is, we now may never know the whereabouts or the fate of young Barnaby Dawe. However, Mr. Walton firmly declared his innocence, so I suppose it is possible that he was not responsible for Barnaby's disappearance. Therefore, the Waskasoo City Police will continue to investigate this case."

"Gaetz Memorial Bird Sanctuary," Patrick repeated under his breath. He shuddered, remembering the cold hand grasping his arm and the dank, choking stench—the smell of river water mingled with the smell of death. It had been the smell of Skip Walton, who had fallen into the shallow water at the base of the cliff.

Thunder rumbled in the distance. Despite what Patrick had said to Nairen, he'd never seriously considered that there might be two ghosts. But now it seemed as if the unearthly hand belonged to Skip Walton, not Barnaby Dawe. The icy touch of a child murderer? Patrick recoiled at the thought.

He quickly scanned the remaining November papers and discovered that the librarian had included half of the December issues in the stack. He found only one more article about Barnaby in the paper dated December 15—brief and no longer front-page material—which informed readers that the police had made no progress in the investigation. Patrick was certain that there would be little else to find if he were to search into 1921. After all, didn't Mrs. Stanier say that Barnaby was never found?

A flash of lightning sliced through the window, momentarily bleaching the newspaper in Patrick's hands. He jumped at the crack of thunder that followed, turning to look out at the storm. The sky was dark, black clouds eclipsing the twilight, and rain began to patter against the glass.

Suddenly, Patrick felt as if he were the only person in the building. The library was deathly still, quieter than even a library ought to be. Patrick anxiously peered down the aisles between the bookshelves, trying to spot another human being. He was sure that if he could see just one other person, the eerie feeling would go away. But he saw no one.

He tried to stand, with the idea of going to find someone, when a powerful force drove him back into his chair. Patrick was immobilized by the touch of two frigid hands. He began to choke as a foul stench filled the room.

Lightning pierced the room again, turning the world a shocking white. Struggling to break free, Patrick turned his head around to face the window. Suddenly the terrible presence was gone, but his throat remained closed. Hovering outside the window, blurred by the rain-streaked windowpanes, was the pale face of Barnaby Dawe.

Time seemed to stop, and in the lull Patrick's thoughts became strangely detached. He calmly wondered about fainting or screaming or running. Instead he did nothing, simply watched in horror as the wretched little creature raised a hand and placed a finger against the damp glass. Slowly the finger moved, pushing the rainwater aside. No raindrop dared fall where the finger had passed. Rivulets of water coursing down the glass changed direction to avoid the letters Barnaby Dawe etched in the wet surface. The word was reversed from Patrick's perspective, but he could read it nonetheless: HELP.

Patrick found his voice. He stood, staring at the window and screaming at the white face.

Chapter Nine

"Young hooligan!"

Patrick stopped shouting and turned to find a walking stick dancing inches from his nose. An old man in a rumpled suit brandished the cane like a sword.

"You know better than to yell in a library. I think you should leave. Now!"

Patrick tried to stammer an explanation, pointing to the window. But only wind-tossed trees, frozen by lightning flashes, were visible beyond the glass. And rain had erased the ghostly writing.

Before he could say anything, Patrick saw

his father moving past the bookshelves. He rushed forward to stand next to his son.

"What's the matter?" he asked.

"This boy—your son, I presume—has been shouting at the top of his lungs. Shouting as if he were on a playground rather than in a library." The old man raised his stubbled chin indignantly. "I've been spending my evenings in this library for twenty years, and I've never been disturbed like this. Never!"

Mr. Meeres turned to Patrick to demand an explanation, but the words stuck in his throat. Patrick was leaning heavily against the table, his body shaking and his face drained of color. Mr. Meeres reached out and placed a hand on his son's shoulder. Patrick's eyes had wandered back to the window, and he flinched at his father's touch. By this time, two librarians had appeared. They stood near the bookshelves, listening.

"I . . . I fell asleep," Patrick said, staring at the floor. "I had an awful dream and then the thunder blasted me awake. I guess I yelled."

The old man's face hardened, and he snorted in disbelief.

"Now look here," said Mr. Meeres, his eyes narrowing. "This isn't the crime of the century. Can't you see the boy's upset? Let him alone."

Patrick's head jerked up in surprise. He glanced gratefully at his father.

The old man glared at Mr. Meeres, then lowered his cane and hobbled away, muttering angrily. The librarians turned away, too.

Patrick scooped up *True Appearances of the Dead,* but left the newspapers on the table. He and his father quickly left the library and darted through the spitting rain to the car. Patrick was relieved that his father didn't ask about the papers. He wasn't up to manufacturing another explanation.

"Bad dream, huh?" asked Mr. Meeres, as soon as they'd settled onto the car seat.

Patrick nodded. He felt a tinge of regret for lying, but knew his father wouldn't listen to the truth. Mr. Meeres was too practical to believe in ghosts. Yet, something made Patrick think his father might understand this time. After all, hadn't he just come to Patrick's defense? But he couldn't bring himself to take the risk. Instead he asked, "Why did you come? I didn't call."

"The library closes in ten minutes, Patrick. You must have slept a long time."

Patrick nodded again, then caught himself off guard by saying, "Thanks, Dad."

Mr. Meeres blinked as an astonished look settled on his face.

"Thanks for sticking up for me."

The mask of surprise slid into a wide grin. "Sure. Glad to help."

Mr. Meeres started the engine, but instead of driving away from the curb, he slapped the steering wheel.

"Sorry, Patrick," he said. "I have to run back to the school for a minute. I forgot to pick up the budget figures when I hurried out, and I need to look them over tonight. Do you want me to take you home first?"

"No, I'll ride along." Patrick did not want

to be alone, not even in his own house. As they approached Craven Hill, silhouetted against bright bursts of lightning, he decided not to wait by himself in the car while his father ran into the building.

Mr. Meeres stopped to unlock and open the driveway gate. It was raining hard as they drove into the small parking lot close to the school.

"I'll just be a minute," said Mr. Meeres, as he reached for the door handle.

Patrick reached for his handle, too, and they opened their doors simultaneously. "I'll come with you," he said.

Heads bent against the wind and slashing rain, they ran toward the girls' entrance. As they drew near, fierce streaks of lightning illuminated the stone steps, and what they saw in the brilliant flash brought them to a stop. One of the tall doors was standing open. In the dim lamplight, they watched the wind toy with the door, rocking it to and fro.

"I know I locked up," Mr. Meeres shouted above a clap of thunder.

They dashed forward, taking the slippery stone stairs two at a time.

"The closing mechanism is disconnected," said Mr. Meeres as he pulled the door closed behind them. "Funny I didn't notice when I was here earlier." He paused, peering through the windows in the vestibule doors. He seemed to be listening for something, but the rain and wind drowned out any other sounds. "The lock doesn't appear to have been jimmied," he said as last. "Still, I suppose someone could be in here. Stay close, Patrick."

A cold feeling crept into Patrick's heart. The door had not been swinging in the wind by accident. It had been standing open for him, and Patrick somehow knew he would have come to Craven Hill that night, had he not come with his father. Even now he was compelled to follow his father into the school, when what he really wanted to do was run back to the safety of the car.

"I think I'll call the police, just to be safe,"

Mr. Meeres said, reaching for a switch that drenched the hall leading to his office in comforting yellow light. "We'll have to wait for them to come."

Suddenly his father seemed like a safe haven. If he could only stay close to him, Patrick felt he might escape whatever was about to happen. He put out a hand to take hold of his father's arm, but his fingers never touched him.

Mr. Meeres continued down the hall, talking as if his son were at his elbow. But Patrick was riveted in place; he could not take a step forward. Against his will, he turned to face the stairs leading to the second story. He opened his mouth to call out, but could make no sound. Instead, he stood in horror, watching as a dark mist rolled down the stairs. Like a great ocean wave it engulfed him, shutting out the light. Then Patrick felt what seemed to be a dozen pairs of hands pulling him toward the staircase. A chill crept from the mist, nibbling at his face and arms.

He fought against the force that dragged him relentlessly forward, but it was a fruitless battle. Soon the tips of his shoes thumped against the bottom stair. Patrick started up the steps, slowly at first, then faster and faster until he was all but running by the time he reached the landing.

As he rounded the landing and started again to climb the stairs, Patrick grabbed the banister and held tight. Then he thrust his arms through the railings and dug in his heels. *I am not going up,* he screamed silently. *I will not go!*

Suddenly he was free. The pressure that threatened to flatten his body was gone. No fingers tugged at him from the dark mist. Patrick pulled his arms from the railings and leaped to his feet. He ran feverishly down the stairs. But as he reached the bottom, he found himself standing instead at the top.

Patrick stood trembling in the cold as the fog rolled aside, revealing the long stretch of hallway leading to the library door. A strange light bathed the hall, and each classroom door stood open like a sentry guarding the way. He turned and rushed down the stairs again, tumbling to the bottom, sprawling on the floor. Patrick looked for his father's office, but he was still staring down the second floor hallway. None of this made sense. He'd fallen down the stairs. *You don't fall up,* he thought desperately. *Has down become up?*

Patrick pulled himself to his feet, then barrelled down the staircase a third time. When he reached the last stair, he finally knew he was beaten. He stood helplessly staring at the library door. The unseen hands began to pull at him again, and Patrick moved down the hall. As he reached each classroom door, it slammed shut as if to say, "Not here." The mist closed in behind him and the cold light faded, leaving impenetrable darkness in his wake.

As he neared the library, the door swung open. He was pulled forward to stand in the opening just as the last glimmer of light disappeared.

Panicked by the total blackness, Patrick struggled to catch his breath. Then, deep within the library, a point of blue-green light began to form, like the flame of a candle springing to life. The flame doubled, then tripled in size, growing until it was twice as large as Patrick. In the light hovered Barnaby Dawe.

The forlorn little figure turned its head toward Patrick, and he recoiled at the sight. The colorless features were horribly contorted by unbridled rage. The phantom's fury stabbed at Patrick, lifting and pinning him against the wall. His feet dangled a foot above the floor.

Barnaby floated forward, stopping an arm's length from Patrick. He did not speak, but his message was clear: *I have waited long enough. Help me now! Help me, or else* . . . The unspoken threat hung in the dark air between Patrick and the ghost. Patrick wanted to cry out, to ask what Barnaby wanted him to do. It wasn't fair to blame him. He didn't know what to do. But Patrick had no voice.

The dark spirit-eyes, like tiny black holes, drank in Patrick's gaze. He felt strength being sapped from his body, flowing from his eyes to Barnaby's, and he grew faint. Then the apparition turned away. The spell broken, Patrick dropped from the air.

Barnaby took several floating steps toward the large, oak map cabinet. He turned once more to catch Patrick's eyes, only briefly, and Patrick saw such a look of pain wash over the little creature's face that he felt like sobbing. Barnaby took several more steps directly into the cabinet and was gone.

With Barnaby went the light. Standing in the darkness, Patrick was unable to move until the bell sounded. Its deep-throated toll reverberated through every board and brick and out into the wet night.

Chapter Ten

Patrick found his legs again and began to back toward the stairs. He had shuffled only a few steps when the overpowering stench of river water and decaying flesh buckled his knees. Icy hands grasped him from behind. He could feel the burning touch of each frigid finger as he was propelled forward through the library door.

Patrick shrieked and was startled by the sound of his own voice. Startled enough to find new strength. He ripped himself from the powerful grip and raced for the stairs. He shook his head violently, fighting the urge to vomit, trying to rid himself of the putrid smell.

He had nearly reached the staircase when his shins slammed against something hard, throwing him to the floor. He shrieked again, and the object in his path cried out, too. Patrick rolled to the side, fighting to free himself from a tangle of arms and legs.

"Patrick."

The voice was barely a whimper, but Patrick recognized its owner immediately.

"Marion? Is that you?"

"Pat . . . Patrick. Get me out. Get me out of here."

The ragged voice, the snuffling, didn't match Patrick's image of Marion. The raw fear exuding from him almost made Patrick forget how scared he was himself.

"What are you doing here?" Patrick whispered as they struggled to their feet and crouched against the banister.

"Get me out of here," Marion pleaded.

"I'll leave you alone for good. Just get me out."

Patrick stood, grabbing a handful of Marion's shirt and tugging him to his feet. "Come on," he said and pulled the other boy toward the stairs.

"The stairs don't work," Marion mumbled. "I tried and tried. But you don't get anywhere. How can we get out?" His voice rose in panic, and his body started to shake. Then his voice dropped so low Patrick could barely make out the words. "What'd we see, Patrick? What'd we see?"

"Never mind that now," said Patrick. He desperately wanted to know if Marion had seen Barnaby, but at that moment, getting off the second floor was more important. "Things are back to normal. I think we can use the stairs again. Come on."

The last wisps of fog curled around the banister and evaporated as they stumbled down the stairs. For the first time since stepping into the mist, Patrick remembered the thunderstorm, but the night was silent except for rain tapping gently against the windowpanes. As they rounded the landing and headed for the bottom, Patrick saw his father.

Mr. Meeres came from outside, yanking open the girls' doors and calling Patrick's name. Before Patrick could answer, his father heard the sound of feet and turned to the stairs. By that time the boys had reached the last step.

"You were upstairs?" Mr. Meeres sounded both relieved and puzzled. "I looked in the car. I never dreamed you'd dare go upstairs again." Suddenly he was angry. "Didn't I tell you to stay close? Didn't you hear the bell? Someone's in here, and he could be dangerous."

Finally Mr. Meeres saw Marion. "Who's this?" he demanded, taking a threatening step in his direction. "Our intruder? Breaking and entering could get you reform school, young man."

"No, Dad, no!" cried Patrick. "This is Marion Trent. I know him. He . . . he came in after we did. Saw the lights and came in. We went upstairs together."

Patrick was shocked that the lie came so easily. But he hadn't lied to protect Marion. Normally, Patrick would have relished seeing the police drag him away—but Marion might have seen Barnaby Dawe.

Marion edged toward the outside doors.

"Oh, no. You're not going anywhere until the police get here," said Mr. Meeres, grabbing his arm.

"Dad! He was with me the whole time."

Marion nodded his head frantically. "I was with Patrick every second."

Mr. Meeres let loose of Marion and stared at his son. "You shouldn't have gone up there," he said absently. A puzzled look crossed his face. "Funny thing, I never knew you were gone. I would have sworn you were with me the whole time. When the bell rang, I looked around and you weren't there.

"Look, I want you boys to wait in my office," said Mr. Meeres, suddenly sounding very much like a principal. "I'll wait by the door for the police. Whoever's in here must be crazy, ringing the bell like that."

"I didn't do anything. Can't I just go home?" Marion asked.

"If Patrick says you're all right, that's good enough for me. But the police may have questions for both of you, so please wait in my office."

Patrick cringed at his father's vote of confidence. It made the lying even worse. But his father's trust also made him feel warm inside.

As the boys reached the office door, the Waskasoo City Police arrived, and they could hear Mr. Meeres explain about the intruder. A moment later, the patrolmen headed up the stairs.

"Did you break in, Marion?" Patrick asked, then immediately regretted his words. Here in the bright lights of the office Marion was the bully again, more threatening now because he had been shamed.

Marion turned cold eyes on Patrick. "Tell anybody about tonight and you're dead."

"But you *were* upstairs before me. Weren't you?"

Marion's eyes narrowed. "I didn't break in. I was cutting across the school grounds, heading home, when I saw the girls' door." He paused.

"I heard this noise, and I saw the door swing open. All by itself! I figured the wind did it, and I went up the steps to look. Then I heard you coming out of the rain. I knew if you saw me, I'd get blamed for breaking in. So I ducked inside and headed up the stairs. . . . Big mistake."

Marion took a deep breath. "I still don't much like you. But I owe you, so I'll lay off—as long as you tell me what's going on."

"I'm not really sure myself," said Patrick, leaning forward anxiously. "Did you see the kid in the knickers?"

Marion nodded. "From about halfway down the hall. I didn't come any closer."

Marion's answer was a double-edged sword. One side sliced away Patrick's fear of being crazy—someone else had seen Barnaby's ghost. But the other side laid open new fears. Nairen could hear Barnaby, and now Marion could see him. Was the spirit becoming more powerful and more dangerous with every appearance?

"Does the name Barnaby Dawe mean anything to you?" Patrick asked. "Or Skip Walton?"

Marion seemed startled. But his features rearranged themselves so quickly, Patrick wasn't sure.

"What? You know about Barnaby? Or Skip?" Patrick slid to the edge of his chair.

"Naw," said Marion. "Never heard of them. Don't want to, either."

"Hey, wait a minute. Aren't you the one who just asked me what was going on?"

Marion's sudden lack of curiosity baffled Patrick. But before he could ask another question, Mr. Meeres and one of the patrolmen walked into the office.

"You boys see anything or hear anything out of the ordinary while you were upstairs?" asked the officer.

The boys shook their heads.

"You two didn't ring the bell, did you?"

"No, sir," said Patrick, crossing his heart.

The officer laughed. "'Cross my heart, hope to die.' Okay, I believe you."

He didn't ask anything else but went back to join the other men who were searching the basement. They had already poked into every space on the second and third floors, where they'd found all the doors closed and locked. Using Mr. Meeres's keys, they'd checked each room. They'd even inspected the belfry and found nothing.

Of course, there was nothing to find

unless Barnaby Dawe chose to reveal himself. The idea made Patrick smile. He imagined the cops crashing down the stairs and out to their cars, speeding off into the night to escape a little boy in knickers.

But thinking about Barnaby soon wiped the smile from Patrick's lips. None of this was funny. Barnaby Dawe had invaded Patrick's life four times that day. Four times, and it was likely to get worse unless he could somehow meet Barney's demands for help. Trouble was, he still didn't know what to do. How could he help when he didn't even know the problem?

The officers had the hardest time explaining away the bell. The bell rope was in a locked closet on the third floor. But it also dropped through the ceilings of the two classrooms directly below the closet, the end dangling in Mrs. Seeley's third grade room on the first floor. Without a key to the closet or the rooms, it would have been impossible to ring the bell.

"Maybe someone hit it with a rock. Or shot it with a gun," a tall, skinny officer suggested. But the belfry was enclosed and far enough from the ground to protect the bell from a rock. And there were no bullet marks on its surface.

Patrick had a feeling the patrolmen still suspected that he and Marion were guilty. And though Mr. Meeres's face was unreadable, he sensed that his father was struggling with the same thought—at least about Marion.

Finally the ordeal was over. The police cars pulled away from Craven Hill, the officers promising to cruise by the school regularly during the night. Mr. Meeres wanted to drive Marion home, but he insisted on walking.

"Ridiculous! Get in the car," Mr. Meeres commanded.

But Marion backed into the darkness and disappeared.

Chapter Eleven

The moment Patrick was alone in his room, he pulled *True Appearances of the Dead* out from under his bed, desperately hoping that it might give him answers about Barnaby Dawe's ghost.

Patrick read late into the night, until he came across several pages that wiped the sleep from his eyes—a section with the heading "Odd Appearances of Spirit Children." Though the book couldn't tell Patrick exactly what Barnaby wanted him to do, it did answer most of the other questions he'd been asking himself. Tomorrow he'd share it all with Nairen.

The next morning, Nairen glanced at the old black book Patrick carried under his arm and whispered questions as they rode to Craven Hill with Mr. Meeres. She was curious about his visit to the public library, even more so because she'd heard the bell toll while she was babysitting. But Patrick made her wait until lunch for answers.

"Too much to tell right now," he said, which only made her more impatient.

By noon, Patrick could see that Nairen was ready to burst. Then, sitting on the bench near the fire tube, he told her the whole story.

Nairen broke the moment of quiet that hung between them after Patrick finished. "Do you think Skip Walton killed Barnaby?"

"I'd say it's a good bet."

"That must be why he's come back," said Nairen. "You know, a guilty conscience." She pointed to *True Appearances of the Dead,* which lay between them on the bench. "I'm sure the book would tell you that's a good reason for a spirit to be restless."

"Well, yes, it does say that. But it also says a lot about vengeful spirits. You know, spirits coming back from the grave to take revenge or cause trouble."

"Could Skip Walton be trying to keep you from helping Barney?" Nairen asked. "Could he hurt you? After all, if he's the killer, maybe he doesn't want the truth to surface."

"He's scarier than Barney, all right," Patrick agreed. "He really pushed me around last night."

Nairen's face clouded, and she stomped her foot angrily. "We've got enough trouble!" she yelled. "We don't need Marion Trent in the middle of this. Plus, that puke got to see Barney when it should have been me. It's just not fair!"

"I've got a feeling you'll get your turn," Patrick said quietly. "If Marion saw Barney, I'm thinking nearly anybody can. Barney's picking up steam, Nairen. I can feel it. It's like he's getting more energy or something."

"But why does Marion have to stick his nose into things?" Nairen complained.

"Well, he promised to leave me alone. So maybe it was a good thing. Scared him off."

"Don't count on it," Nairen grumbled.

"There's something more to tell you," said Patrick. "I saved it for last."

"There's something else?" Nairen sat up straight and moved closer.

Patrick picked up *True Appearances of the Dead*. "There's a section on ghost children. It explains a lot of things about Barney, like how children who die lonely or violent deaths seem to have more energy, more power than other spirits. More than adults who die in the same way. And their power grows when humans pay attention to them."

This seemed to catch Nairen's interest. "Like power to appear on a movie screen?"

"Or whisper along with the Everly Brothers," said Patrick. "There have been lots of incidents of ghost children moving heavy objects or pulling nails from the wall. And one ghost managed to print her picture in a book someone was reading. Once in a while a child spirit has so much raw energy he can pull a human right into his own time."

Nairen looked puzzled.

"I know, it sounds impossible, but the book told about a boy in the 1890s who disappeared for nearly a week, then was found wandering around the English countryside in a daze. He said he'd been taken home by a strangely dressed child with a bluish face and a terrible gash on his forehead. The child lived in the castle perched on a nearby hill, only that castle had been in ruins for five hundred years!"

"Okay, Barney's powerful," Nairen said slowly. "So why can't he use his power to clear the air? Tell you straight out what he wants? Or help himself, for that matter?"

"Even though child spirits appear as if they can do anything," said Patrick, "there seems to be a boundary they can't cross. The book says they are 'governed in their power.' Apparently they cannot directly help themselves, and they can't ask for specific kinds of help. Here, listen to this."

Patrick leafed through *True Appearances of the Dead,* and then began to read:

These unfortunate young souls may cryptically point the way to their unhappy resting places but ultimately are forced to rely upon earthly beings to unravel their mystic clues and find their final remains. This state of affairs may lead to violent displays of impatience and frustration if the living helpmeet is slow to solve the puzzle.

"Unhappy resting places? Is that what Barney wants?" Nairen cried. "For you to find his body?"

"I think so. By the way, did you ever wonder why Barney waited thirty-eight years? The book says that spirits often sleep until something happens to awaken them, and it told about a case in Scotland. I guess a boy disappeared from his family estate and was never found. A hundred years later workmen were rebuilding part of a stone wall that surrounded the estate. At the same time, the spirit of a child began appearing to another young boy in a nearby village. As it turned out, the boy convinced his father, who was working on the wall, to tear away a certain section. They found the child's body sealed inside."

"Yuck!" Nairen stared at Patrick in horror. "That's sickening."

"The point is that something stirred Barney's spirit."

"The earthquake?"

"That's what I think, too. These spirits want to be released from their 'spiritual bondage,'" Patrick said. "That means a ghost is chained to the spot where it died. Usually if its body can be found and moved to a family burial plot, that does the trick."

"But then why is Barney leading you to the library? Skip Walton couldn't have killed Barney and hidden him there. The police would've found evidence. And there's no place to hide a body."

"But maybe there's a clue in the library. A hint to point us somewhere else," Patrick suggested.

Lunch was nearly over. They ate quickly and returned to work, vowing to keep their eyes open for a sign from Barnaby Dawe.

Mrs. Stanier had Patrick move and re-shelve books while she and Nairen began an inventory in another part of the library. Working alone allowed Patrick to think about what he'd suggested to Nairen, that the library held a clue to Barnaby's secret. But where? More than once, Patrick stopped working and looked around him, hoping for inspiration. Then he remembered watching Barnaby vanish into the map cabinet.

Patrick strode over to the cabinet, which sat at the end of a row of floor-to-ceiling bookshelves. He pulled out the top drawer and riffled absently through the maps and posters inside. Then he checked the underside to see if something might be taped to the bottom.

I've been reading too many mysteries, he thought, feeling a little foolish. Still, Patrick looked in and under each of the six drawers, finding nothing. He put his shoulder against the cabinet and pushed, but it wouldn't budge. Patrick thought about taking the drawers out and looking inside. But Mrs. Stanier had already noticed him lingering around the map cabinet, so he casually wandered back to his workplace.

When Mrs. Stanier called it quits for the day, Patrick was still in the dark, though he now felt strongly that the cabinet held the secret. He remembered again Barnaby's angry impatience and grew cold inside. Patrick shivered, fighting off his mounting fear, for suddenly he knew that Barnaby would force him back to the library that night. His room would offer no protection. He would be drawn to the school. The girls' entrance would be standing open in the black air, waiting for him.

Once again, Nairen and Patrick were finished before Mr. Meeres was ready to leave, so they walked home. As they pushed through Nairen's screen door, Mrs. Potter's cheery call rang from the kitchen. "Hi, kids. Come take a look."

She was at the table, the paint-by-numbers propped before her on an easel. "It's nearly finished," she said, "but it's still *quite* mysterious."

Nairen and Patrick came around behind Mrs. Potter, peering over her shoulder at the mystery canvas. For a moment, the room swirled around Patrick, and he reached for the back of Mrs. Potter's chair to steady himself. Barnaby had finally pointed the way.

Chapter Twelve

Only a few of the numbered spaces on the canvas were without paint. Mrs. Potter had done a careful job; the images were clear and sharp. The scene showed a narrow, paneled wall at the end of a row of floor-to-ceiling bookshelves. A large cabinet sat to the side, as if it had been pushed away from the wall, and a pale little boy, dressed in knickers and a shirt with a sailor's collar, stood with both hands spread against the paneling. He looked over his shoulder with dark eyes that seemed strangely alive. No matter one's angle to the painting, Barnaby Dawe was watching every move.

"Great work, Mom." Nairen couldn't keep her voice from squeaking.

"Why, thank you, dear." Mrs. Potter sat back in her chair, examining the painting with a tilted head. "I expected a farm scene or maybe a copy of some famous painting like the Mona Lisa. But this is so odd. What does it mean?"

No one answered.

"Well," said Mrs. Potter cheerily, "how about a snack? There's a box of Popsicles in the freezer. Or some chocolate cake left over from dinner last night."

Nairen and Patrick chose Popsicles and headed outside where they could talk. She erupted the second they cleared the screen door. "It's just like that ghost you read about, the one that printed its picture in someone's book. Can you believe it? Barney put himself in a paint-by-numbers. Is that really what he looks like?"

"Not so loud," Patrick whispered, glancing back inside the house. "That's exactly how he looks. *Exactly.*"

Nairen pulled Patrick toward the street. When they reached the curb, she continued in a loud voice. "You already knew about the map cabinet, didn't you? I saw you sniffing around it this afternoon."

"Barney disappeared into that cabinet, remember? So I thought it was the best place to start looking."

A light went on behind Nairen's eyes. "But Barney didn't really disappear into the cabinet at all. He disappeared into the wall behind the cabinet." The light faded. "But there can't be anything behind that wall. Maybe a little empty space between the bookshelves—that's all there's room for."

Patrick plopped down onto the curb. "Look," he said, crossly, "if Barney says look behind the wall, what choice do we have?

Besides, maybe all he wants us to do is look *at* the wall."

"I didn't mean we shouldn't look. It just seems so weird."

"Everything that's happened is weird, Nairen." Patrick took a bite of his Popsicle. "Trouble is, I don't think we can move the cabinet. I tried to slide it this afternoon, and it weighs a ton."

"Let's ask your dad for help," Nairen suggested.

"No! No way." Patrick shook his head emphatically.

"Patrick, give him a chance. I know he'd help us."

"You don't know anything!" Patrick stood angrily, then sank back to the curb with a sigh. "After last night, Dad knows somebody was in the school, but he refuses to believe that has anything to do with my seeing a kid on the second floor. We can't chance it. He'd stop us, Nairen. I'm sure of it."

"Okay, okay. We'll do it ourselves." Nairen wrinkled her nose thoughtfully. "Maybe if we took out all the drawers. Take out all the drawers and what've you got? Nothing more than a big empty box."

Patrick was stunned by her simple solution. "That's great, Nairen. Beats my idea of renting the Waskasoo High football team."

Nairen laughed.

A car horn honked, and they looked up to see Mr. Meeres pulling into the driveway next door.

"Hey, there, kids," he called as he stepped from the car.

"I thought you were staying late," Patrick called back. He and Nairen stood up and walked toward the car.

"I decided to go back for a while this evening. Hope you don't mind," his father answered. "There are plenty of things for me to do at school, and I really wouldn't mind being there to discourage prowlers."

Despite what he'd told Nairen, Patrick felt a sudden longing to confide in his father. But he swallowed the urge, quickly thinking of a way to get his father's help without telling him anything.

"How about letting Nairen and me come with you?" Patrick asked.

Mr. Meeres looked surprised. "But you spent all day at Craven Hill. Why in the world would you want to go back?"

"Uh . . . Nairen lost her necklace, probably in the library. We want to look for it."

"You'll be through looking long before I'll be ready to leave," Mr. Meeres warned.

"What if we brought Monopoly? We could play in the library until you're finished."

Patrick could feel Nairen's eyes boring into him, but he refused to look at her. He excused the lie by telling himself that this was an emergency. That they had to get a shot at moving the map cabinet before Barnaby lost all patience. *And besides,* Patrick told himself, *Dad is happier not knowing.*

"Well, I suppose so," said Mr. Meeres. "A few more lights in the building might help keep our unwanted visitor away. But there'll be no horsing around, understand?"

"No trouble, I promise," said Patrick.

Nairen's parents thought playing Monopoly in the school library sounded like fun, so they readily agreed to let her go along. After supper, Patrick ran next door to get her. Nairen stepped out of the house with a Monopoly box under her arm, just as Mr. Meeres pulled up at the curb.

"I don't remember you wearing a necklace, Nairen. Do you usually wear one?" Mr. Meeres asked as they drove along.

"Uh . . . no. But I did today." Nairen aimed an evil look at Patrick.

"Well, I hope you find it," said Mr. Meeres.

When they reached Craven Hill, there was still plenty of sunlight, and the old school didn't seem as threatening as it had the night before. Mr. Meeres ushered Patrick and Nairen through the girls' entrance. Once inside, he checked that the door was locked and then marched up the stairs to open the library.

"Happy hunting," he said, switching on the lights. "See you in a couple of hours."

As soon as Mr. Meeres was gone, Nairen rounded on Patrick and said, "Don't you ever make me fib to your father again."

Instead of answering, Patrick hurried to the map cabinet and pulled on one of the drawers. It rolled out on clacking ball bearings, and he began examining the drawer's tracks to see if it could be removed.

"You know, the bookshelf is wider than I thought," said Nairen, as Patrick fiddled with the drawer. "The cabinet must be about five feet across, and it only sticks out about six inches on each side. That means the bookshelf is four feet wide."

"So what?" said Patrick.

"There are shelves on both sides, but they're only . . ." Nairen walked over to the shelves and reached in to touch the wood behind the books. "Only about nine or ten inches deep. That means there's more than two feet in the middle."

Patrick looked up from the drawer. "Two feet?"

"Yeah. Which means there's plenty of room for something behind the paneling—something good-sized."

Patrick blinked, then turned back to the cabinet. His hands were shaking.

"Come on, help with these drawers," he said. "Lift up and then pull, and they'll come right out. They're heavy, so it'll take one of us on each side."

They opened the bottom drawer and lifted it out together.

Nairen groaned. "Who knew maps could weigh so much," she complained as they set the drawer on the floor next to the cabinet.

As they bent to lift out the second drawer, Patrick and Nairen heard footsteps in the hall. Expecting Mr. Meeres, they jumped up guiltily. Patrick was already fumbling for an explanation when Marion Trent stepped through the door.

"What are you doing?" Nairen demanded. "Does Mr. Meeres know you're in here? Well, does he? You're going to be in big trouble, especially after last night."

Marion's eyes flashed angrily at Patrick. "You were supposed to keep your trap shut about last night," he growled.

"Nairen can keep a secret."

"Go get your dad," Nairen urged, tugging on Patrick's sleeve.

Marion smiled. "But daddy already knows I'm here."

"The doors are locked, so how'd you get in?" Nairen asked fiercely. "Break a window?"

"I'm legal."

"I'll bet," Nairen said.

"Look, I stood outside your old man's office window and yelled until he saw me. He wasn't too happy at first. But when I told him I'd come to play Monopoly with my good friends Patrick and Nairen, he let me right in. No questions asked."

"But . . . but how'd you know about the Monopoly?" Patrick asked.

"You know those big lilac bushes in your front yard? Well, I was in them. Heard every word. Find your necklace, Potter?"

Nairen snorted. "You're such a creep. Let's go get your dad, Patrick."

"Look, Patrick . . . I couldn't sleep last night," Marion said. "And I was so scared just now, I could hardly climb those stairs again. But I climbed them anyway, 'cause I have to know what's going on."

"Forget it!" Nairen grabbed Patrick's arm. "Come on, let's get your dad."

"Okay! Okay. I'm sorry. Sorry for . . . well, you know." Marion stared at the floor.

"Yeah, we know all right." Nairen's eyes blazed. "And we still don't trust you and that little snake that follows you around. By the way, where is the snake? If you're here, he can't be far behind."

"Danny?" Marion said absently. "I ditched him. Patrick, maybe I can help."

"We need to move that map cabinet," Patrick said.

"Patrick," Nairen hissed. "Don't do this."

"It'll be okay, Nairen."

She glared at Patrick, then wheeled around and stomped over to one of the tables, collapsing into a chair.

Marion perked up. "Sure, I'll help. But what's the cabinet got to do with . . ."

"The kid in the knickers?" asked Patrick.

Marion nodded.

"First thing you should know, that kid's been dead nearly forty years."

Marion's face turned chalky. He nodded for Patrick to go on. So Patrick told him about Barnaby's disappearance. About the incessant hauntings from both Barnaby Dawe and Skip Walton. About the first solid clue that might help them put the unsettled spirits to rest.

"That's it! You've heard enough." Nairen

stood abruptly. "We don't have much time. Get those drawers out," she ordered.

Without a word, Marion and Patrick set to work while Nairen supervised. Soon all six drawers were out, and Marion threw his weight into the cabinet, trying to slide it.

"Won't move," he grunted.

Nairen dropped to her hands and knees. She peered inside the empty box and groaned. The boys joined Nairen on the floor.

"It's anchored," said Patrick, examining the large brass brackets and screws that held the map cabinet solidly in place. "We'll need a screwdriver."

"Well, we don't have one," Nairen said. "And we can't very well ask your dad to raid the janitor's closet."

Suddenly a cold, damp breeze swirled around them. The faint smell of decay filled the room, and Marion started to shake. His eyes began to roll back into his head, and Patrick thought he was going to pass out.

"Grab him," Patrick yelled.

Nairen took one of Marion's arms and Patrick the other. They forced him to his feet and pulled him toward the door. The stench of rotting flesh hit them full force, and all three gagged. Still, Patrick and Nairen half guided, half dragged Marion toward their only route of escape.

As they reached the doorway, a strange squeaking noise brought them to a stop. The sound was coming from the cabinet. At that moment, the horrible smell dissipated and with it went some of their fear. With Marion in tow, Patrick and Nairen crept back.

When they drew near, Nairen sucked in her breath. They watched as one of the large brass screws squealed and creaked as it unwound itself from the hardwood floor. Then the screw toppled and lay gently rocking in a fine layer of white dust.

Chapter Thirteen

Wide-eyed and silent, they watched all eight screws free themselves from the floor. Then Nairen knelt and plucked the screws from inside the cabinet. She handed them to Patrick as Marion pointed to the floor. A trail of water snaked from the doorway, puddling in a dark pool near the map cabinet. Nairen dipped her fingers in the water and lifted them to her nose.

"Smells terrible," she said, grimacing. "Like dead animals."

Patrick turned away from the pool and dropped the screws on a table top. "Okay, let's move this thing," he said, his voice tight.

The map cabinet popped loose from the floor with a tiny cracking sound and then slid easily. Careful not to scratch the floor, the three of them eased it to the side just far enough to uncover the wall at the end of the bookshelf.

Patrick approached the dark wood panel-ing, which looked exactly like every other paneled wall in the library. It was four feet wide and consisted of two oak panels, one on top of the other, that rose to the ceiling. Each panel was recessed in thick oak trim, beveled like a picture frame. The trim kept the map cabinet from sitting flush against the wall, allowing thick layers of dust to accumulate. Other than an assortment of candy wrappers, spit wads, and paper scraps, there was nothing else behind it.

Oak knobs, rounded and a little larger than a silver dollar, decorated the center of each panel. They graced the other panels in the library, too, but Patrick hadn't noticed them until now. The knobs were embossed with the image of a stately manor house that looked very much like Craven Hill School. Patrick guessed it was Craven Hill Manor, the mansion in Arthur Paginet's favorite mystery novel.

"What now?" whispered Nairen.

Patrick started tapping on the paneling, and Nairen took his lead. She stepped forward and began tugging on the oak trim. Because of the tall ceilings, Marion had to pull a chair over to the wall, stack some dictionaries on it, and then stand on top of the stack to reach the second knob. Patrick instructed Marion to try pulling, pushing, and turning the oak knob while he did the same to the one below. But all their rapping, sliding, pulling, and turning yielded nothing. The oak paneling and trim were solid.

"It *does* sound hollow, don't you think?" said Nairen, but the more they tapped, the harder it was to tell. They tapped on other walls, trying to compare the sounds. In the end, every panel began to sound the same.

Suddenly, Patrick kicked over a chair in disgust. "What are we supposed to find?" he cried, looking at the ceiling.

Leaving the others behind, he rushed back to the wall hidden so many years by the map cabinet. He stood silently, waiting for a sign. His eyes combed the paneling, re-examining every square inch and watching for something to happen.

"He's probably gone as far as he's allowed," said Nairen, coming to stand next to Patrick. "We have to do the rest."

"But this isn't getting us anywhere," said Patrick, and once more he turned his eyes to the ceiling. "Do you hear me, Barnaby Dawe? Show me the answer. Do whatever you want with me. I don't care anymore. Just show me!"

The lights flickered, and an icy breeze swept through the library, sending the old paper scraps and candy wrappers spiraling. The wind wrapped around Patrick and held him for a moment in its cold embrace, fill-ing his heart with a strange mixture of dread and joy. Then the frigid air leaped from Patrick and burst across a row of books, throwing them from the shelf.

"You asked for it," Nairen said quietly. "I hope you're not sorry."

Without another word, they slid the cabinet back into place and tossed the screws inside before replacing the drawers. After straightening the library, they set up the Monopoly board, playing mechanically until Mr. Meeres came for them.

When Patrick went to bed that night, he sensed that Barnaby's power had increased tenfold since he'd granted the spirit absolute control. But right or wrong, it was done, and Patrick wasn't sorry. He was ready for whatever Barnaby Dawe had in store.

Patrick was still awake when the plaintive toll of the bell rolled across the rooftops of Waskasoo City. He would never hear it ring at night again.

* * *

A patrol car was cruising by Craven Hill when the solitary peal of the bell cut through the darkness. In minutes, the building was swarming with blue uniforms. But the offender had managed to elude them once again.

When Nairen and Patrick arrived for work the next morning, the police were back, hoping daylight would uncover a clue hidden by the dark. Patrick wished he could tell them not to waste their time. Nairen, on the other hand, thought it was funny.

"You just can't fingerprint a ghost," she said, laughing under her breath. "But maybe they'll find some ectoplasm stains."

Patrick gave a half-hearted smile. He was distracted by a tightness in the air. It was like the heavy stillness preceding a violent storm.

Mrs. Stanier had them continue the job of gluing in card pockets and attaching labels. Meanwhile, she busied herself in the storeroom.

"Any more from Barney last night?" Nairen asked the second they were alone.

Patrick shook his head.

Nairen shifted uncomfortably in her chair. "I don't like this, Patrick. It's like the rules have changed. Aren't you worried?"

Patrick shrugged. "We may need to get into the school tonight," he said. "Whatever's going to happen will most likely happen right here."

"Is your dad working late again?"

"No. He's going to a meeting. Maybe Marion can get us in."

"Oh, sure," said Nairen, rolling her eyes. "He'll have us jimmying the locks. You know, it's not like the police aren't watching the place."

"I hate to admit it, Nairen, but he was a big help last night. That is, after he got over Barney's trick with the screws."

"And Skip Walton's juicy aroma," Nairen added, a hard edge to her smile. "I loved seeing him sacred silly. Loved it! It felt like we were getting back at him for all the rotten stuff he's done to us. Didn't you just love it, Patrick?"

"I guess so."

"You guess so? Come on, this is Marion Trent we're talking about."

"We need his help, Nairen. And I did promise to let him know when we were going back for another look."

Nairen wagged her head in disbelief. "Okay. It's your funeral, Patrick Meeres. Don't say I didn't warn you."

"I'll call him when we get home," said Patrick, as though he hadn't heard a word she'd said.

"Maybe you should check in the lilac bushes first," Nairen said.

Patrick grinned as he opened a new copy of *Old Yeller* and began to attach a card pocket. But the book slipped from his fingers, which suddenly had no feeling in them, and fell to the table while Patrick's unfocused eyes gazed into space. Cold air seeped into his shoes, sending tendrils up the legs of his jeans. Then he felt something pushing against his shoulder, and his eyes focused to find Nairen nudging him.

"Hey, Patrick. Wake up."

"Was I asleep?" he asked, groggily. "I had a dream, I think."

Nairen peered anxiously under the table as the cold air nibbled at her ankles. "About Barney?" she asked.

Patrick shook his head. "I was twirling around in the dark. Dropping down and twirling around. I thought it would last forever, and I was so cold. But then I saw a light, and I flew out of the dark into the sunshine. That's when you jabbed me."

"You wouldn't answer. I didn't know what else to do."

"Come with me," Patrick said. He stood up and called to Mrs. Stanier. "We'll be right back."

The librarian poked her head from the back room and waved.

"What are you doing?" Nairen stumbled after Patrick. "What's going on?"

"It's time to 'do the tube,' Nairen."

"Are you nuts?"

"Isn't that what it's like when you slide

down the tube? Like my dream?" asked Patrick.

"Well, sort of." Nairen seemed confused. "But your dad's the principal. No principal in the world will let you 'do the tube' for fun."

"It's what I'm supposed to do, Nairen."

She stepped out of Patrick's way and then followed him down the stairs. "I don't know about this, Patrick," Nairen said.

"I do," he answered.

A moment later, Patrick tapped on his father's office door.

"Hey, you two." Mr. Meeres looked up from the pile of papers on his desk. "Aren't you supposed to be working?"

"Dad, we want to slide down the fire escape."

"What? 'Do the tube?'" Mr. Meeres's smile faded, but then he laughed at the surprise on Nairen's face. "Didn't think I knew about 'doing the tube,' eh? Well, word gets around. And the answer is 'no.'"

"It's summer, Dad. No one's around, and Mrs. Stanier goes home for lunch." Patrick could feel his father weakening. "Just once, that's all."

Mr. Meeres looked ready to say no again, but he shivered at a momentary chill in the air and seemed to lose track of his thoughts. Instead he looked back and forth between Patrick and Nairen. "Okay," he said slowly. "A couple of times. During lunch when Mrs. Stanier is gone."

"Thanks, Dad."

"Yeah, thanks a lot, Mr. Meeres."

"Now you two get back to the library. I'll see you at noon," he said, waving them out of his office.

"How'd you do that?" Nairen asked as soon as they were back in the hall. "I couldn't believe my ears. He wanted to say no. You know he did."

"All I did is ask," said Patrick.

The rest of the morning crawled by tediously. Finally, Mrs. Stanier headed home for lunch. Patrick and Nairen found Mr. Meeres waiting for them on the steps leading to the third floor.

The third floor's large open area doubled as a lunchroom and recreation hall. Deep storage closets lined the north and south walls, except where a set of wide doors entered the room. Tall windows and fire escape doors were located to the east and west.

They walked across the floor, footfalls echoing in the emptiness, and came to the east fire escape exit. Patrick's father pushed open the door. A narrow, caged catwalk bridged three feet of air between the building and the green tube. The height was dizzying.

Mr. Meeres seemed reluctant to step out on the catwalk. "Afraid of heights," he said apologetically. "Have you done this before, Nairen?"

She nodded. "During fire drills."

"Then show Patrick. I'll go down and

unlock the bottom door and wait there to catch you. Don't start down until I say so."

After Patrick's father left, Nairen began giving instructions. "You go first," she said and herded Patrick onto the catwalk. He, too, was a little afraid of heights, and a delicious tingle of fear tickled his midsection.

"Pull open the door," she ordered.

Patrick pulled on a handle, and a section of the tube opened like the hatch on a space capsule. A breath of stale, chilled air puffed from the tube, and they both shivered.

"Are you sure you want to do this?" Nairen asked, a troubled look clouding her face. She peered past Patrick at the shiny, cylindrical slide that wound away into the dark.

Patrick blinked. "No choice," he said.

"Okay, then . . ." Nairen took a deep breath. "Sit with your legs sticking downward. Then push off and lie down with your arms crossed over your chest to keep them out of the way."

Patrick sat down in the opening, his legs

resting on the slide. The metal was cold, even through his jeans. Too cold for summer.

"Okay," Mr. Meeres called from below.

Patrick pushed off, crossing his arms as instructed. As he picked up speed, the sense of falling caused a rush of adrenalin. Immediately, he was flung into the dark, his body riding high on the curves of the slide. Up and down, left and right meant nothing in the frigid darkness. This was exactly like his dream.

After more than a minute had gone by, Patrick realized that he'd been spinning downward far too long. The light at the end of the tunnel never appeared, and the cold became numbing. Then, without warning, Patrick flew out of the tube, his landing cushioned by a pile of fallen leaves. He lay staring into the moonlit sky of a crisp, autumn night.

Chapter Fourteen

Patrick sat up, looking around in wonder. He clutched himself against the cold; his jeans and T-shirt were no match for the freezing temperature. A half moon peeked from behind a trailing cloud, yet the dark sky was mostly clear and star-spangled. Patrick noticed that the surroundings of the school were different than he remembered. The new playground equipment was gone, and the large oak trees that lined the east side of the school grounds were so small that they were barely visible in the moonlight.

He stood and took a few steps forward when he felt the panic rising inside. It had been a mistake, a terrible mistake, to have given Barnaby this much control.

Swallowing his fear, Patrick was determined to fight back. He quickly decided that his only chance was to climb up the slide in hope of finding his own world at the top. He turned toward the tube, but to his horror, it was gone. Patrick remembered that the stairs of a regular fire escape clung to the other side of the building. Maybe he could get back to the third floor that way.

Patrick ran past the boys' entrance and skirted the school. He noticed for the first time that the leaves made no sound as he pushed through them. He kicked at them purposefully and stamped on them, but his foot traveled silently through the dried husks. Suddenly Patrick realized that he no longer felt the cold. He plucked at the bare skin of his arm and did not feel his own touch. Then Patrick held his hand between his face and the moon. Faint blue light passed through his flesh as if it were no more than a clouded piece of glass. It was as if he didn't exist.

As he rounded the building, he saw that the other fire escape was gone, too. His only way to the third floor was through the school.

Patrick stopped in front of the girls' entrance. Again, he saw differences as he gazed around the dark school grounds. An ornamental garden that sat beside the building was missing. He had run right through the empty space. In the light that shone above the entrance, he could see that the doors looked newer and that the school's wooden trim was green rather than brown.

He approached the stone steps, feeling strangely calm. Something important waited inside—something more important than reaching the third floor. Patrick shivered with unexpected excitement.

He stepped impatiently onto the first stair, but his foot passed into the stone. He cried out, his cry soundless. Patrick backed away from the stairs, then tried again. With all his effort, he concentrated on the steps and on his feet. He quickly learned to keep himself on top of the stone steps, barely floating above them. Patrick made his way to the doors and reached for the great iron handle. His arm sank into the wood, disappearing up to the elbow.

Why fight it, he thought. *I'm the ghost here.* Patrick closed his eyes and walked through the wood. The sensation was strange, like a mild electric current, but when he opened his eyes again, Patrick was standing in the vestibule.

He had already noticed lights shining from within Craven Hill School. Someone was inside. Passing through the next set of doors, Patrick moved toward his father's office. As he neared the door, he saw a bearded man in a dark, three piece suit and a bow tie sitting at the desk—a larger, more ornate desk than his father's. The man wore gold-rimmed wire glasses, and a gold watch chain looped across his stomach.

He was studying a sheaf of papers, but suddenly his head jerked up. He stared nervously at the open doorway, and Patrick knew he'd been caught. But the man's eyes peered through him for several moments, then returned reluctantly to the papers.

Patrick knew what he was seeing—or rather, whom. His heart began to beat rapidly. This was Abner Dawe.

Patrick turned and drifted toward the staircase. He floated up the stairs, faintly aware that the wooden steps were not as cupped and worn as he remembered. When he arrived on the second story landing, Patrick stopped, hovering in confusion. He vaguely remembered wanting to reach the third floor, but then he was distracted by the light. The door to the Paginet Library stood open, the brightness from inside flooding the dark hall.

This is 1920, murmured a voice inside his head. *November 18, 1920.*

Patrick's stomach clenched. He didn't want to go into the light, and yet he knew he must. He glanced at the staircase and was lured by the third floor and its promise of escape. But Barnaby was waiting. Not the ghost child but the real boy, and Patrick knew he could not abandon him. He started toward the light.

He stopped in the doorway, squinting against the brightness, and then stepped into the library. A small face looked up from a book, gazing through Patrick and out into the hall. Patrick caught his breath. He couldn't help himself. After seeing the tortured, angry spirit of Barnaby Dawe so many times, Patrick wasn't prepared for this pleasant, happy child.

Barnaby's table was scattered with books. He was holding *The Wizard of Oz,* and his eyes returned to the pages.

Patrick stood very still, nervously awaiting events he was sure he didn't want to see. It was hard for him to imagine that these peaceful moments were likely the last moments of Barnaby's life. He kept peering over his shoulder, looking down the hallway for Skip Walton.

Suddenly, Barnaby sighed and tossed his book aside. Bored with his reading, he stood up and began to wander idly about. Patrick moved forward, his eyes searching behind shelves and tables. Fear knotted his stomach. If he spotted Skip Walton lying in wait, there was absolutely nothing he could do, nothing but watch history take its course. He fought the urge to rush from the library.

But Patrick didn't find Skip Walton. He hurried to the door and peered down the hall again. No one. Then he turned his attention back to Barnaby.

Barnaby's eye seemed to catch something interesting, and he stopped at the end of a bookcase, staring at the paneled wall. Patrick gasped. Why hadn't he noticed earlier? Barnaby stood right where the map cabinet should have been; there was no cabinet in 1920.

Patrick drew closer as Barnaby extended his hand and tried to grasp the decorative wooden knob on the lower panel. He was barely able to get his fingernails under its edge. He pulled and twisted, but it did not budge. If Marion couldn't move the knobs, Patrick was certain that someone as small as Barnaby had no chance.

Barnaby reached into the pocket of his knickers and pulled out a good-sized pocket knife. He unfolded the blade and began to pry on the knob. Patrick realized that he was trying to pop it off, and, indeed, the knob shifted forward slightly. The movement energized Barnaby, and he began prying vigorously. The knob eased away from the wall half an inch.

Now Barnaby was able to get his fingers around the knob, and with a solid grip, he yanked with all his eight-year-old might. The knob pulled out six or eight inches. It was somehow attached to a metal rod that protruded from the wall.

The smooth sound of precision machinery reached Patrick's ears as the knob snapped back into place. In an instant, both panels disappeared up into the ceiling. Barnaby jumped backward in surprise but then crept forward curiously.

Behind the panels, a narrow flight of stairs marched upward into the darkness. The stairs were two feet wide, or perhaps an inch or two wider—precisely the space Nairen predicted they would find between the shelves. The other bookcases were easily as thick, but Patrick guessed that the others harbored no secrets. They had been built just as wide in order to keep this particular shelf from standing out.

Barnaby peered into the secret passageway, Patrick right at his shoulder, and found an old-fashioned light switch on the wall. He pushed one of the two buttons. A single bulb, suspended from the ceiling, snapped on, revealing an open doorway at the top of the stairs.

Patrick was confused. What did this have to do with Skip Walton? With Barnaby's disappearance? Yet, somehow he sensed that Barnaby shouldn't go up the stairs, shouldn't go through the doorway. He turned and floated out into the hallway, checking in vain for Skip Walton. Then he hurried back to follow Barnaby.

The stairs were empty, and Patrick concentrated hard in order to climb them. They were so narrow that some full-grown men would have had to turn sideways. When he reached the top and stepped through the door, he found Barnaby standing in the center of a small room. It was no more than ten by ten feet, with a ceiling seven feet high. Patrick realized that this secret room was ingeniously wedged between two floors, probably extending out into the false towers that decorated each side of the building.

The walls of the room were brick. The ceiling was a steel plate, and though the floor was hardwood, Patrick guessed it was laid over another thick sheet of metal. Bookshelves lined two walls, and a padded wooden bench ran along the third wall. A row of ornate brass lamps, attached to the bricks, hung above the bench. Barnaby stepped over to the lamps and pulled a dangling cord. The room blazed with light.

Patrick followed Barnaby to the bookshelves and began reading the titles. They were all Gothic mystery stories, including several copies of a book titled *The Haunting of Craven Hill Manor.* This was Arthur Paginet's private joke—a library within a library. His own secluded, but most likely never used, refuge. Patrick was certain that the idea of a secret room must have delighted his sense of the mysterious.

Barnaby began pulling books from the shelves and looking behind them, as if he expected to find a hidden compartment or something equally intriguing. He had just cleared an entire shelf when the whisper of well-oiled rollers caused him to freeze. As suddenly as the secret door below had opened, another door at the top of the stairs slid from within the wall, sealing the room with a deadly click.

Barnaby screamed and ran to the door, pounding on it with his fists. Then he began frantically searching for a lever or knob—a release mechanism that would set him free. The door was a smooth sheet of steel, so he attacked the wall, running his fingers across the bricks. But there were no knobs or hidden switches to trip the latch. Barnaby screamed again, tears coursing down his face. He kicked at the door, crying for help.

A sob stuck in Patrick's throat. He watched in agony as the tiny figure searched wildly about the room. The mask of terror and despair that cloaked Barnaby's face was frighteningly familiar. It was the face on Barnaby Dawe's ghost.

Chapter Fifteen

Finally, Barnaby collapsed to the floor, weeping bitterly, and Patrick knew it was time for him to go. Leaving tore at his heart, but to stay would accomplish nothing. He was powerless in this place and time.

Reluctantly, Patrick passed through the door, immediately discovering that another thick panel had dropped from the ceiling midway down the stairs. The panels at the bottom of the steps had also rolled back into place, creating a soundproof barrier between Barnaby and the outside world.

Patrick moved through the wall and into the library, pausing to look at the wooden knob. He wished he had the bulk to pull the rod and open the doors. He even made a feeble attempt to take hold of the knob. But, of course, it was no use. And it was no use trying to communicate with Abner Dawe. Even if Patrick were able to draw him to the library, it would be impossible to show him the hidden door.

All that was left for Patrick to do—all that he could do—was find a way home. He hurried away from the library, hoping that the third floor would send him back to 1958. At the top of the great staircase he stood for a moment, afraid to see what lay on the other side of the doors. Patrick steeled himself and floated forward. But as his head emerged into the room, his heart sank. He'd hoped to find Nairen waiting on the catwalk, wondering when it was her turn to start down the slide. Instead, the recreation hall was dark and cold.

Patrick floated across the empty floor to

the eastern windows and peered out. The moon cast shadows across the school yard, and there was enough light for him to see that the side of the building was bare. The tube was still missing.

For the second time in minutes Patrick felt a sob stick in his throat. He was trapped, stuck somewhere between life and death. He wondered if his days were to be spent aimlessly wandering the halls of Craven Hill School, wandering through thirty-eight years until a summer day in 1958 would bring him home again. Or was he to spend eternity in the shadows of this November night?

Suddenly, Patrick felt an uncontrollable urge to leave the building, to go back outside. He turned with purpose and whisked out of the recreation hall and down the stairs. Without pausing to glance in Abner Dawe's direction, he headed into the vestibule of the boys' entrance and through the outside doors. As Patrick stood on the east side of the school, he saw a line of flickering blue lights like moonbeams reflecting from a pond. The tube materialized before his eyes.

At that moment, Patrick heard feet shuffling through the dead leaves, and he looked toward the sound. A rumpled man staggered out of the night and stopped near the bottom of the stone stairs leading to the boys' entrance. Patrick was nearly close enough to touch him.

Light from the doorway caught the man's haggard features, and Patrick drew back from his angry scowl. His eyes were unfocused, and he teetered as he stood. Then he raised a drunken fist, shaking it at the doors.

"Damn you, Ab . . . Abner Dawe," the man whispered, his speech slurred. Without another word, he turned and shuffled on.

Patrick seemed frozen until Skip Walton disappeared from sight and the rustle of dried leaves fell silent. When the night was still again, he flew to the tube's dark opening and flung himself inside.

Moments after he entered the tube, Patrick was "real" again. He felt the chill of cold steel as he splayed himself in the slide. He gripped with his hands and feet and began to push himself upwards. But when Patrick rounded the first turn, something crashed into his head and shoulders. His grip broken, he was forced back down the slide while Nairen's surprised yelps echoed in the spiraling shaft.

Connected like train cars, Patrick and Nairen shot out of the tube and into the blazing summer sunshine. They fell in a derailed heap at Mr. Meeres's feet.

"What the . . . ?" Mr. Meeres jumped back involuntarily, then rushed forward to help untangle Patrick and Nairen. "You should have spaced yourselves. Going down together like that was dangerous," he scolded. "Are you all right?"

"I'm okay," said Nairen. "How's your head, Patrick?"

Patrick reached up to touch his forehead

where Nairen's shoe had scraped away the skin. He grinned and winced simultaneously. For the first time in his life, Patrick was happy to feel pain. The stinging sensation and the smear of blood on his fingertips told him he was safe. Safe in his own body and in his own time.

"Get that stupid grin off your face," said Mr. Meeres, irritably. "Here, take my handkerchief and hold it to your head. It's just a scrape, so it won't bleed much."

"Uh, Dad . . ." Patrick gingerly dabbed his forehead with the hanky. "Don't blame Nairen. We didn't come down together. I used the soles of my tennis shoes to slow myself down. I don't know why, I just did."

Patrick looked at both his father and Nairen, a wide grin back on his face. "Sorry," he said.

"You don't look very sorry," said Mr. Meeres. "It was a dumb thing to do, Patrick."

"Yeah, pretty dumb," said Nairen. She rubbed a sore elbow and glared at him.

"I said I'm sorry."

"Well, I guess I'm sorry, too," said Mr. Meeres. "Sorry I let you talk me into doing this. Run up and close the door at the top. I'm going to lock up down here."

"Okay, Dad. Come on, Nairen."

Patrick pretended not to notice Mr. Meeres's look of relief. He knew his father had expected a disagreeable response—a peevish retort or brooding silence. Patrick grinned again and started for the boys' entrance.

As soon as they were inside the school, Nairen thrust her scraped elbow in front of Patrick's face. "Why'd you do it?" she hissed.

"I didn't."

Nairen stared at him coldly. "You think that's funny?" She turned away and walked up the stairs.

"I went all the way to the bottom," Patrick said, hurrying to catch up.

"And your dad never saw you because you climbed back in so fast. Patrick Meeres, faster than a speeding bullet."

"Stop it!" Patrick yelled. "I went all the

way to the bottom, but when I flew out of the tube, it was nighttime. Dad wasn't there. You weren't there. It wasn't even summer anymore. It was dark, and it was autumn."

Nairen stopped and stared at Patrick. Then she ran up the stairs, leaving him behind. By the time he reached the third floor, Nairen was out on the catwalk closing up the tube. He waited in the middle of the floor until she was done.

"I came out in 1920, Nairen," he called across the recreation hall. "Just like the English kid and the castle, only I went back to November 18, 1920. I saw what happened to Barney."

They sat on the top stair near the entrance to the recreation hall, and Patrick told Barnaby's story. Nairen swiped absently at a tear trickling down her cheek but didn't say a word until he was finished.

"It's awful," she said when Patrick fell silent. "What an awful way to die. Being alone and scared and hungry for days. And then . . ." Her voice faltered, and she dropped her head into her hands.

"I know," said Patrick. "But that's the whole point—he doesn't want to be alone anymore."

Nairen raised her head. "We need to let his family know what happened. He's got to have relatives around somewhere, don't you think? We'll just have to find them. I bet he wants to be with his folks again. You know, buried in a family plot, like the book said. And we need to let everyone know that Skip Walton was innocent."

"Finding what's left of Barney will automatically let Skip off the hook," said Patrick. "Then he can rest in peace, too. I guess he's here to help Barney, not to hurt anyone."

"Just think," Nairen whispered, gazing at the stained glass in the stairwell windows. "All that time you spent watching Barney. All that time and yet I ran into you seconds after you started down the tube. Weird." She looked at Patrick and smiled. "You were a ghost. You traveled through time. Why does all the good stuff happen to you?"

"Hey, Meeres. Over here."

Patrick squinted into the twilight. Marion's voice came from the lilac bushes at the corner of the house. "It's nearly dark, Marion. No one's going to see you visiting a nerd."

"Yeah, well, you can't be too safe." The bushes rustled, and Marion stepped into the warm summer night. "Danny knows I'm here," he said. "So I guess I wasn't careful enough, was I? Sneak a look at the light pole over there."

Marion jerked his head toward the street corner. In the yellow circle of light, Patrick could make out a small figure pressing himself against the pole.

"Must've followed me." Marion smiled. "Maybe I'll have to punch you. You know, so no one will suspect anything."

Patrick stepped back, and Marion laughed. "Just kidding. So what's this you said on the phone? The kid's dead body is trapped in a secret room? Sure you aren't just dreaming?"

"What do you think?" asked Patrick.

Marion scuffed the toe of his tennis shoe in the grass. "Guess I've seen enough crazy stuff lately that I'd believe anything. So, if the kid locked himself in a room that means Walton didn't do him in? Right?"

"That's right."

Marion smiled. "That's good. And you figure if we open up this room and get the kid's bones out, the haunting stops?"

"Makes sense, doesn't it?" said Patrick.

"Yeah. Yeah, it makes good sense. So you need me to get you into the school after dark."

"No one's going to believe the truth, Marion. What grown-up is going to let us move the map cabinet and start prying on the wood paneling? We have to do it when no one's there to stop us."

"Cops'll be thick as mosquitoes," said Marion. "But I've got an idea."

"What?"

"No way." Marion waved his finger in the air. "I'm not telling you just yet. I've got to think on it some more, and I'm going to need tomorrow to get stuff ready. You and Nairen meet me right here, tomorrow at midnight. Your folks ought to be sleeping by then. And bring flashlights."

"I hope Barnaby can be patient until then," said Patrick.

"I figure he knows we're coming," said Marion. "He's waited a long time. One more day won't much matter, as long as he knows we're on our way. See you tomorrow night."

"Wait! What do we do about Danny?"

Marion stepped forward quickly and shoved Patrick hard enough that he lost his balance and fell into the grass. "That should take care of it," he said. With a smile, he slipped behind the bushes and was gone.

Chapter Sixteen

Patrick lay in the dark listening to his father get ready for bed. He heard the toilet flush and the water run in the bathroom sink. Mr. Meeres was up later than usual, and Patrick looked nervously at his alarm clock. Eleven-twenty.

By 11:30 the house was dark. Patrick breathed a sigh of relief. His father usually read in bed, sometimes for hours, but tonight he turned out the lights right away. Patrick listened for the slow, rhythmic breathing that would be his signal for escape. But Mr. Meeres coughed, tossed and turned, even got up once and walked over to his dresser for something.

Go to sleep. Go . . . to . . . sleep, Patrick willed his father.

It was midnight before Patrick felt it was safe to leave the house. Already dressed, he rose from his bed, slipped on his shoes, and grabbed his flashlight. His father snored gently as Patrick crept down the hall and out the front door.

Nairen and Marion were waiting by the lilacs. They blended into the bushes, and Patrick was worried when he didn't see them. But as he drew near, two dark figures stepped into the pale moonlight. Patrick noticed that Nairen was standing at least six feet away from Marion.

"You're late," Marion complained. "Okay, follow me." He gestured with his head and disappeared into the bushes.

Patrick and Nairen pushed between two lilacs and into the backyard. Marion was already standing in the alley, waving them forward.

As they joined him on the gravel, Marion pointed to the soft glow of the light poles along the street. "No lights back here. Best we stick to the alleys so no one will see us."

"How do we get into the school?" Patrick whispered.

"It's all set." Marion grinned. "While you two were in the library with old prune-face Stanier, I waltzed right into the school and up the stairs. If Patrick's dad had spotted me, then I was coming to see you. But he didn't, so I hiked up to the recreation hall where I fixed things for tonight."

"What'd you fix, Marion?" Nairen asked, impatiently. "How're we getting in?"

"Keep your shirt on, Potter. You'll see when we get there."

Marion turned on his heel and darted down the dark path. He stayed to one side of the alley, slinking along fence lines and weaving among trash cans. Patrick and Nairen hurried to keep up, straining to see what lay in their path and feeling strangely like criminals. They dodged from alley to alley, working their way toward Craven Hill School.

The last two blocks they were forced back to the streets because the alleys didn't run in the right direction. They had just started through the rear gate of the school grounds when Nairen pulled the boys behind one of the oaks that bordered the walkway. A black-and-white squad car rolled by a moment later.

"Good job, Potter," Marion said.

Without another word, Marion moved to the walkway. With Patrick and Nairen in his wake, he veered toward the girls' entrance, but stopped before they reached the doors.

"Here we are."

In the faint light from the moon, Patrick saw that Marion was looking at the other fire escape. He hadn't noticed it in the dark because the ladder-like stairs, which criss-crossed the side of the building, stopped ten feet above. The bottom set of steps was suspended in the air, parallel to the ground, and held up by a system of weights and pulleys. That way, no one—including kids at recess—could climb the fire escape from below. But when people came down the fire escape, their weight caused the last set of steps to lower slowly into position.

"Are you a kangaroo?" Nairen asked, tartly. "Because it'll take a heck of a jump."

"Watch," said Marion.

He stepped to a nearby hedge and pulled a long bamboo pole from underneath. Puzzled, Patrick and Nairen watched as Marion began to poke at the bottom step of the fire escape. Suddenly, a coil of rope, which had been impossible to see in the dark, tumbled down, unwinding as it fell.

"The fire escape doors in the recreation hall aren't locked on the inside," Marion explained. "I crammed a matchstick in the works so the door would shut but not latch. I had the rope with me in a paper bag, so I ran down the fire escape and tied it to the bottom step. Of course, that lowered the stairs, and it was tricky to balance the rope so it didn't fall off when they raised back up."

"Brilliant," said Patrick, staring in awe at the dangling rope. "Really, Marion. It's a brilliant plan."

Marion smiled. "Grab hold," he said, taking the rope in his hand.

Together they pulled until the stairs lowered enough for Nairen to hoist herself onto the steps. The boys scrambled aboard, and Marion untied the rope, coiling it and slinging it over his shoulder. Then they hurried up to the first metal landing. Without their weight, the stairs swung upward again.

At the top of the fire escape, Nairen pulled on the door, and it came open easily. Marion stopped to pry loose the piece of wooden matchstick, and the door closed with a click.

"Remember, no flashlights yet," Marion said. "Don't want to tip off the cops."

Enough moonglow filtered through the windows to help them across the recreation hall and down the stairs. It was darker in the second-floor hall, but they were still able to feel their way along.

Just as they reached the library, Patrick stopped short. "Oh, man! The door's locked, Marion. And you can't break the glass, if that's what you're thinking."

"Be quiet," Marion growled. He moved to the door, his form silhouetted against the window.

Patrick and Nairen couldn't see what he was doing, but they heard the sound of metal against metal. Then there was a heavy, metallic thunk, and the library door swung open.

"You stole a key!" Nairen said.

"Look, my pa used to work with locks, before he ran off," Marion said. "This is an old fashioned bit-type lock. It uses a skeleton key. The trouble with skeleton keys is that there aren't enough variations. Back in the old days, a key might open several houses in town.

"Most of the school doors still have these old locks, and we got a whole box of skeleton keys at home left over from pa. In fourth grade, I started bringing a different key every day, and when nobody was looking, I'd try 'em on all the doors."

"You found one that fit the library," said Patrick.

"You got it. I already knew I could get us into the library if I could figure how to get us into the school. So I didn't steal any-ing, Potter."

Suddenly the familiar stench of river water and decaying flesh swept through the library door. Marion yelped and jumped back into the hall.

Patrick peered into the library while he tried to cover his nose. "Our friends are get-ting impatient," he said.

The smell faded, and Patrick strode purposefully toward the map cabinet, dropping his flashlight on a nearby table. He opened the top drawer just as Nairen joined him. Together they lifted it out and set it on the floor.

Marion was still standing in the doorway, sniffing the air. Patrick and Nairen were struggling with the second, heavier drawer when he began to come slowly in their direction. He looked rapidly right and left as he crept forward and finally arrived in time to help with the third drawer.

When the cabinet was emptied, Nairen reached inside and picked up the screws they'd thrown there two nights before. Then they slid the cabinet aside. Patrick felt his stomach flutter as he stood before the wall, his eye on the oak knob in the center of the lower panel. He reached into his pants pocket, pulled out his Swiss Army knife, and unfolded the largest blade.

"Well, here goes."

He wedged the cutting-edge of the blade under the knob and pried upward. It didn't budge.

Nairen drew closer. "Maybe it stiffened up over the years," she suggested.

Patrick tried again, pulling fiercely. Suddenly something popped, and at first he thought the blade had snapped. Then he realized that the sound was the knob releasing. Now it stood out from the wall about half an inch.

Patrick pocketed his knife and, with a claw-like grip, wrapped his fingers around the knob and tugged. A metal rod slid out of the wall several inches. Then the knob was jerked from Patrick's hand, slamming back into place, and the panels disappeared into the ceiling.

Chapter Seventeen

Until that moment, Patrick wondered if the light in the hidden stairwell might have burned steadily for thirty-eight years. It had not, and the inky blackness that greeted them made the moonlit library seem bright by comparison. Though the night was warm, a breath of cold, stale air wafted from the dark hole that yawned before them, and all three shivered. They stood rooted in front of the opening, hardly daring to breathe.

At last, Patrick noisily pulled in a deep breath of the stale air, breaking the intense silence. He handed Marion his knife. "You stay here to open the panels. Nairen and I will hurry, but we could get caught inside."

"Giving orders now?" Marion tried to sound miffed, but Patrick could tell he was relieved. "Okay, I'll wait here. I'm surprised you trust me, Meeres. Maybe I'll leave you locked up with Barney."

"Wouldn't be a smart move," said Patrick, "because I'd come back to haunt you."

"Me, too." Nairen laughed. "Not to mention Barney."

"Get going. I don't have all night," Marion said nervously.

Patrick retrieved his flashlight and then probed with his foot to find the first stair. "I'm leaving my light off until I'm inside," he said as he started upward. "Just to be safe."

Nairen followed closely. "Talk about narrow," she whispered. "Hurry, Patrick. If I think about this much more, I'll chicken out."

After a few steps, Patrick flicked on his flashlight, and the cramped stairwell seemed a little less threatening. Then the beam from Nairen's flashlight shone over his shoulder and penetrated the shadows at the top of the stairs. Patrick stopped, and his knees weakened at the sight of the next dark opening, gaping like the maw of a giant beast. What was left of Barney waited just beyond.

Nairen nudged Patrick's shoulder with the tip of her flashlight, and he started moving again. But when they reached the top of the stairs, both of them hesitated, pointing their lights at the ceiling instead of into the room. The air was tainted with a hint of Skip Walton.

The faint smell of river water and festering flesh shook their resolve, and Patrick backed down a step, bumping Nairen and causing her to stumble. She grabbed at his shirt to steady herself. When Nairen had regained her balance, she poked Patrick in the ribs.

"Hey, watch it."

"Sorry. I'm scared, Nairen."

"Me, too." She gently pushed him forward. "But we have to do this."

They stepped through the doorway, their flashlights still aimed at the ceiling. Patrick lowered his beam, directing it carefully toward the bookcases and away from the bench. Nairen did the same.

Only a thin layer of dust covered the scene revealed by the narrow shafts of light. All the books were pulled from the shelves and lay scattered on the floor. Patrick knew that Barnaby had stripped the bookcases in his wild search for the doors' release mechanism. He also knew that Arthur Paginet wouldn't have designed the room without a way to open the panels. But wherever the knob or lever was located, Barney hadn't found it.

Unable to delay any longer, Patrick turned his beam toward the reading bench,

Nairen's following. The instant the light touched the bench, Patrick squealed and dropped his flashlight, which winked out as it hit the floor. He'd known what to expect, and yet it had taken him by surprise. Nairen sucked in her breath.

Barnaby's skull grinned at them from the corner of the seat. Tufts of dark hair still clung to the white bone. His torso, covered by the shirt with the sailor's collar, also rested on the bench, but the earthquake had loosened one set of arm bones which lay broken and scattered on floor. Legs had fallen from the seat, too, and lay part in and part out of his knickers. Both feet were encased in the heavy, high-topped leather shoes, but one foot had broken free. The shoe had rolled away from the bench, the foot bones presumably still inside.

Patrick and Nairen stood in awed silence, staring at the pitiful little piles of clothing and skeletal remains. Starving and weak, Barnaby had lain on the cushioned bench and given in to death. But first he had searched his prison for a way to escape, torn the books from the shelves and felt every inch of the brick wall. He had screamed and cried and prayed. But finally he was beaten, and there was nothing left to do but curl up and die. Alone and afraid.

Their morbid reverie was suddenly disturbed by the sound of a door easing shut behind them. Even though they knew Marion would open the panels for them, Patrick and Nairen felt a surge of fear course through their bodies as the door clicked into place. It wasn't much of a click, but it was the sound that had sealed Barnaby's fate. An odd sense of doom settled over them, and they moved closer to each other for comfort.

Seconds ticked by, and the door did not open. As Patrick felt Nairen cling to his arm, he fought against the panic rising inside him. Why wasn't Marion opening the panels?

Suddenly, Nairen's flashlight began to dim until its light faded away completely. They moaned in unison, overwhelmed by their terror and by such total blackness. The smell of water and mold and death intensified, filling the room and gagging them. Flecks of moisture carrying the stench sprinkled their faces. Patrick and Nairen stumbled backward until their shoulders rammed against the door.

As they pressed against the metal, they watched two dull, blue-green globes of light appear, one on each side of the bench. The globes brightened, pulsated, and grew into long, irregular forms. Within the light, figures began to materialize until the clear images of two people stood before Patrick and Nairen. Shrouded in the blue-green light, the tiny figure of Barnaby Dawe clutched the edge of the wooden bench and stared forlornly at his own bones. The other figure was a man, dripping wet and shivering. A puddle gathered at his feet, a

rivulet running toward the door and stopping just shy of Nairen's shoes. Patrick recognized the face of Skip Walton, the man
he'd met on the school yard that cold
November night.

Skip Walton also gazed sadly at Barnaby
Dawe's skeleton. It was as if neither specter
had noticed the living souls who shared the
small room with them. Then, together, the
spirits looked up at Patrick and Nairen.
Slowly, a smile crept across each luminous
face, and the evil stench disappeared.

A reassuring calm filled Patrick, driving
away the terror. He smiled in return, keenly
aware that the mask of anger and fear had
melted away from Barnaby's face. Barnaby
was the happy child he'd found reading *The
Wizard of Oz*.

The blue-green lights faded, and with
them the figures of Barnaby Dawe and Skip
Walton. The last thing Patrick saw was Barnaby's head nod in his direction. It was

meant to say thank you. And to remind Patrick to finish the job.

As soon as the ghost glow was gone, the flashlight in Nairen's hand began to burn faintly, strengthening until its beam cut through the blackness. The door at their backs whisked into the wall, and they walked calmly down the stairs.

Police cars ringed Craven Hill School in the predawn shadows. Nairen stood near the girls' entrance with her parents, bathed in the red gleam of flashing lights. Nearby, Patrick leaned against his father. Marion had slipped away.

Patrick was surprised that none of the adults, including the police, appeared to be angry with them for breaking into the school, for handling the whole affair on their own. The grim discovery, along with its odd and unexplainable circumstances, seemed to have disarmed any criticism. Even Mr. Meeres had little to say, and Patrick sensed that his father was struggling with the truth—struggling to come to grips with the blue-green boy he'd scoffed at a few nights earlier. Despite his father's troubled silence, Patrick was comforted by the strong arm that circled his shoulders.

Everyone stepped back as the funeral car from Gaetz Mortuary drove up to the door. Two patrolmen carried a long bag down the stairs and slid it gently inside the hearse. The driver pulled away into the fresh glow of sunrise.

Chapter Eighteen

Patrick rushed out his front door, slamming it behind him. Nairen waved from her porch swing, and he hurried toward her, giving Marla and her Hula-Hoop a wide berth.

"Guess what?" Patrick said breathlessly, as he dropped down beside Nairen. "Dad got a call from the police earlier this afternoon. They've tracked down Barney's family."

"Finally!" Nairen hopped off the swing. "What took them so long? It's been two whole weeks!"

"Barney's father and younger sister both live in Chicago. Can you believe it? Abner

Dawe is still around. Chief Lassiter told dad that they cried and cried, right over the phone. They'll be here the day after tomorrow to take Barney home. He'll be buried in Chicago, next to his mother."

"Finally at rest," Nairen murmured, sitting down again. "And Skip Walton, too. We did a good thing, Patrick Meeres."

"Yes, we did," Patrick agreed. A smile touched the corner of his lips. "We even found Mrs. Stanier another storage room."

Nairen laughed. "But Mrs. Stanier's so short. She'll need a step ladder to reach the door switch." Her voice turned somber. "Even if he'd known the switch was behind a false brick, Barney was too small to reach it."

"Maybe if he'd stood on a stack of books," said Patrick.

"Yeah, maybe."

They sat in silence for a few minutes, watching as the mailman came around the corner, working his way from house to house. Soon he was handing Nairen a stack of letters and left Patrick the Meeres's mail, too.

When the postman was gone, Patrick shuffled through the mail until he came to a letter with his name on it. A spidery hand had addressed the envelope to Master Patrick Meeres.

"Is that for you?" Nairen asked.

Patrick looked puzzled. "The return address says it's from the Parkland Retirement Center. Who would I know there?"

He ripped into the envelope and pulled out a single sheet of stationery. Several lines of the same shaky handwriting snaked across the page. The letter read:

12 August 1958

Dear Patrick,

My name is Mavis Tilden. You don't know me, but I know you since reading all about you and your friends in the

newspaper. Thank you very much for what
you did. You have taken a great weight off
my weary old shoulders.

Sincerely,
Mavis

It was late afternoon before Patrick and
Nairen pedaled their bikes onto the grounds
of the Parkland Retirement Center. The
two-story retirement home was nestled into
the slope of West Hill and offered a com-
manding view of Waskasoo City.

When they asked the receptionist about
Mavis Tilden, she sent them out onto a
large covered veranda that overlooked the
river valley. Several elderly men and women
sat at tables playing cards or dominoes, and
a line of rocking chairs stood like sentries
guarding the porch railing. An attendant in
a nurse's uniform pointed to a tiny woman
with snow-white hair who was bobbing back
and forth in one of the rocking chairs.

"Mrs. Tilden?"

Watery blue eyes captured the two young visitors and held them for a moment. "You must be Patrick Meeres," the old woman said. Her voice was surprisingly deep for such a dainty body, and a little scratchy. "And you must be Nairen Potter. I know you're not Marion because Marion is a boy!" Mavis's pleasant laughter rang out across the veranda.

"You know Marion Trent?" asked Nairen.

"That I do. He's my grandnephew. Thanks to Marion, I know even more about you than the newspapers told me. He visits me every week. I had no children of my own, you see, so little Marion is like my own baby."

Patrick and Nairen smiled as they imagined Marion's reaction to being called a baby, even by his own great aunt.

"I suppose you're here to ask about my letter," Mavis continued.

"That's right," said Patrick.

"Well, now, that letter was as much Marion's idea as mine. We decided that if my little note made you curious enough to come for a visit, that I would tell you a secret about Marion and me. And here you are!" Mavis leaned forward. "Do you know what my maiden name is?" she asked suddenly.

They shook their heads.

"Why, it's Walton."

"Walton!" Patrick gasped. "Skip Walton?"

"Terrence was my younger brother." Mavis stared across the valley, lost in thought. Then she turned to look at her visitors. "I loved him fiercely, but poor Terrence always seemed to court trouble. Not big trouble, mind you. But then he started drinking—he was always ornery when he was drunk. Gave guff to everyone who crossed him, including Mr. Abner Dawe. I knew bigger trouble was coming his way. Just the same, it broke my heart when the town accused him of kidnapping that little child."

"Did *you* think he'd kidnapped Barnaby?" Nairen asked.

"Terrence wasn't violent. He just talked violent when he was liquored up. No, I never believed he hurt that boy. And now we know for sure that he didn't. Some old-timers have never completely forgiven our whole family for what they thought Terrence did to Barnaby Dawe. But now . . . well, thank you both."

Tears trickled down Mavis's wrinkled cheeks. She reached forward, taking each of them by the hand. "Thank you," she said again, giving their fingers a grateful squeeze. Then she sat up straight in her rocker, looking deep into Patrick's eyes, and into Nairen's. "Marion says you saw Terrence. How did he look?"

Patrick and Nairen looked at each other in surprise.

"You really believe we saw ghosts?" asked Patrick.

"The veil between this life and the great beyond gets thinner every day for someone my age," said Mavis. "What you experienced is no surprise to me. Now, tell me about Terrence."

"He *was* a ghost, Mrs. Tilden, so you can't expect too much," said Nairen. "He was dripping wet and looked awfully cold, but he smiled at us. I'm sure he knew the truth was finally out in the open."

Mavis sighed and leaned back in her chair.

"We'd better head home, Mrs. Tilden," said Patrick. "Our parents don't know where we are."

Nairen stood up. "But we'll come back for another visit. If that's all right."

"All right? Why I should say so. You come any time."

As Patrick and Nairen started down the veranda steps, Mavis called them back.

"Oh, Patrick, one more thing. I'm a mite worried about you." Mavis lowered her voice.